WHAT HE WANTED

JADA PEARL

Jessica Watkins Presents

Acknowledgements

This book is dedicated to my angels: my parents Billie and
Ernest Jr., and my twin sister, Meco and my grandparents Billie
Mae, Calloway, Jean and Felton. Thank you for continuing to
watch over me always. Love you and RIH!
My struggle for staying strong has been tested, but without God
I would be absolutely nothing! So I am giving God his much
deserved praise for waking me up daily and giving me an
opportunity to get it right and create.

I want to thank my sons, Quentein (Nylah) and Alvin Jr. for
always being so supportive of my work. I love you both. To
Gloria,Tricia, Darenda, Latonya, Ta-Nisha, To-Nesha, Ashley,
Octavia, Tyra, Tina, Nina, Sonia, Monique, Joy M., Jay, Dani,
Kenya N, Kenya R Isis M : you all have been my lifeline at
some point. Special thank you to my constant muse. Thank you
to the rest of my huge family and friends for the encouragement
and support.

Jessica & JWP, where would I be without the strong love and
unit you have all provided?! Family is what you all are!

Special thanks to Tenita, Cynthia and Danielle M: you rock.
Last, but not least, thank you always to my readers for sticking
by me and being patient as I create.

Hannah
I have to introduce myself
to your readers, I hope
you fall in love with
Jada Pearl's style like I
have in creating her style
Bromance - never stop
believing in HEA!.
Jada Pearl

ALEXIS

A lexis opened her door, dragging her tired body into her house. She threw her purse on the table and hit the light switch. She was surprised when the room didn't flood with light. She walked over to the lamp to check the light bulb, but stopped short when she heard a noise behind her. Turning, she screamed when she came face to face with Sean Edwards.

"Hi, baby. You miss me?" He placed his hand over her mouth to keep her from screaming again. He grabbed her before she could try to get away. Pinning her to the wall, he spoke with his face close to hers. "Don't fight me because this can get ugly if you want it to."

Alexis saw the evil in his eyes and slowed her struggling down. She tried to think quickly, but she also didn't want to set him off again.

"Now, if I take my hand off your mouth, you promise not to scream again?"

Alexis nodded and Sean slowly lowered his hand, but not before trying to kiss her. Alexis' stomach turned as he continued to try to get her to return his kiss. She moved her face to the side.

"Sean. Sean, please stop. Why are you doing this? Why are you here?"

Sean stopped and looked at her smiling. "I told you, you would be mine no matter what, and I am not going to give up until you are!" he spoke defiantly.

Alexis didn't dare say what she was thinking. This man was crazy.

His eyes traveled down her body and she instantly felt dirty.

"Sean, you're hurting me. Can you please let me go?" she pleaded with him and he gave her a look she couldn't read.

After a few moments, he spoke to her, it wasn't roughly, but it still felt like he was putting needles in her as every part of her body felt like it was being pricked.

"No, you are up to something. We are good like this."

Sean grabbed her hair, pulling hard as he tried to use his other hand to fondle her breasts. They struggled for a few minutes.

"SEAN STOP!" she pleaded as the tears clouded her vision and wet her face.

He stopped and looked at her for a second.

"You know you want this just as much as I do," he told her as he increased his grab on her. His laughter filled the silence as he continued his attack on her, tearing her blouse.

She screamed again, but for some reason her scream didn't actually come out of her mouth, and the room suddenly got quiet. She could feel the fear and how much tension was in the room. Everything seemed to move in slow motion for the next few minutes as Sean leaned down to try and kiss her again. Alexis continued trying to get out of his grasp. They both were breathing hard from the struggle. Suddenly, they were quiet before the sound of a phone ringing cut into the silence. They looked at the other.

⚜

ALEXIS OPENED HER EYES WITH A START. SHE LOOKED AROUND confused. She still heard the ringing. Realizing it was her alarm clock on her cell phone; she reached over and turned it off. She lay back down and wiped her face with her arm. This was the third time this month that she had dreamed about Sean. She didn't like it one bit. Just laying there thinking about the dream was causing her head to throb. "Ugh" she spoke aloud to the quiet room, turning on her side she was greeted by a slim vision of the sun through her windows' blinds. Sean had caused her enough pain. Exasperated she willed herself to get up, even with her now uneasy stomach. Changing her thoughts, she let her mind go to Zavier, her boyfriend, as she passed the picture frame of them together. Zavier was a stocky built man that stood a good foot over her average height frame. Bowlegged, he had a walk that had a few women stop what they were doing just to watch. His smooth skin was the color of chocolate milk, with a dimple in his left cheek that housed a rugged beard. He wore small diamonds in his ears. He had just recently decided to let his fade haircut grow, she still didn't know how she felt about it, she preferred the low cuts.

Stepping out of her night shirt, she looked at her five-foot five reflection in the bathroom mirror. She wasn't thick and she really wasn't skinny, she had a nice butt, but could stand to hit the gym more. Running the back of her hand over her cheek, Alexis admired her skin which had the color of toffee; she had almond shaped eyes and semi full lips. Her hair was in locs, she'd had them for the last five years, and she loved their texture. Growing up she was always mistaken for her mom when she was living. She favored both her parents actually. Her eyes were brown with small specs of gold just like her dad.

Her dad. Today was his death anniversary. Two years he had been gone; she wished both of her parents could be here today. Her mom had died ten years earlier from a heart attack; it caught her and her dad off guard. It was a process, Alexis wiped her eyes absently and saw that her hand was wet. She didn't even realize she had been crying. At that moment, she was glad Zavier wasn't there. He would want her to talk about her current emotions, and the bad dreams that kept her turning and tossing all night, but she intentionally avoided the conversation to prevent revealing that part of her past. She still wasn't ready yet. But she knew she wasn't going to be able to keep this up, he could feel something was up with her, and it was much more than the nervousness and excitement of the studio opening today.

ALEXIS' LIFE WAS ABOUT TO CHANGE, HER NEW DANCE AND YOGA studio, Infinity in Motion was opening today. She had chosen this date because of its significance in her life. Even if it was bad, she had to start somewhere. It had taken her years to get to this point, and nothing was going to stand in her way, not even her bad dreams, thoughts, and pain. She needed to put her big-girl panties on and push everything else to the back of her mind.

After showering, she chose her outfit carefully. She would be conducting tours before her classes began that evening. She was making breakfast when her phone went off. She smiled as Zavier's face appeared on the screen.

"Good morning, Zav," she greeted.

"Good morning, beautiful. How are you doing this morning?"

"I had a hard time earlier, but I am thinking good thoughts."

"I'm glad to hear that. I wish you would have let me stay last night. I was up worried."

"I know, but I was up all night getting ready. I didn't want you disturbed by all that."

"Okay. I won't make a big deal as long as you're good."

"Thank you, Zavier."

"So, I will meet you at the studio if that's cool with you."

"Yes, we should be all done around eight."

"Oh, I have a surprise for you."

"A surprise, huh? Well, you know I love surprises. Let me finish this breakfast and I will call you this afternoon."

"Okay, baby. Be careful on your drive. I love you!"

"Love you too," she told him before they ended their call.

The phone call with Zav had her mind racing as she strolled into the kitchen. Mindlessly, Alexis took a bite of her buttered, wheat toast, wondering what his surprise would be. They had been dating for over a year now, and she couldn't have asked for a better man. Zavier had been recently promoted to the athletic director at Sinclair Community College. They met at a fundraising event. They had hit it off but decided to date lightly in the beginning. However, after about three months, things changed and they began dating exclusively. Zavier was romantic from the start, and she loved that about him. They used to spend hours on the phone just talking, he always gave her something to look forward to when they met up, he was always attentive to her, and she reciprocated. It was the first time a man outside her father had such an impact in her life.

Walking to her car, she scanned the street. She had a weird feeling she was being watched, but she didn't notice anything in her immediate vision. Dismissing the feeling she got in car, waving to her neighbor that was coming off his porch as she pulled out of her driveway... Deciding to take the local streets of Detroit, she let her mind wander. Her studio used to be her dad's security office; he held gun safety classes and lectures on the importance on gun control. She had gutted out the back, adding a whole wall of mirrors for the actual studio area. The walls were painted a soft blue, yellow and gray. She hoped the butterfly mural had been hung as she instructed. It used to be her mom's and she had some pieces added, and was excited to see what it looked like. Downtown Detroit was bustling as she pulled into the newly painted parking lot.

Entering through the back entrance, she immediately let her eyes travel around the studio. Her vision was coming alive and she immediately felt excited; walking towards the front, she saw the men hanging the mural as Amber, her assistant, instantly greeted her. She handed her several message slips. Alexis casually flipped through them. She glanced into the reception area, where the finishing touches were being done and the last-minute details were completed. They had under two hours before the doors would open. She had a busy day ahead of her which included a scheduled interview with the local channel six news, studio tours, and hopefully, a bunch of children and adults who would register for dance and yoga classes.

Alexis walked over to where one of the male workers was adding lighting. While giving directions, she finally noticed some of the flower arrangements that were already neatly placed on one of the tables. She touched the petals of one, briefly reading one of the cards. She cupped her mouth and tried to keep her emotions stable. She was humbled and grateful that her old staff members from the community center would show her so much love. She had almost made it to the end when a deliveryman brought in a huge arrangement that was covered up.

He looked down at his clipboard. "This is for Alexis Morgan," he announced.

"Oh, that's me! Do you need me to sign something?"

"Yes, please." He placed the arrangement on the table with the others. Alexis signed as instructed, handing the clipboard back to him, and continued to finish what she had just started at one of the other tables, leaving the arrangement for Amber to handle when she returned to her desk.

WITHIN MINUTES, AMBER RETURNED FROM THE BACK WITH A FOOD tray in her hand. Walking carefully, she placed the tray on the table that included several other trays of food, refreshments, and the give-aways in the corner area of the lobby. Stepping back, Amber admired her decorative work. Glancing over she noticed the covered arrange-ment, "Did you want me to unwrap this one?"

"Yes, please I didn't want to mess up your arrangement of every-thing so I left it for you." Alexis told her with her back to where Amber was. Turning, she smiled as Amber smoothed her skirt. Amber was about five feet, four inches, a dark complexioned woman whose glasses always were at the tip of her face. She had her hair in a tight clean bun, and looked every bit of the classic receptionist role. Coming out of her thoughts, she walked over to the table, "Do you need any help with anything before I go into my office?"

"No, I think I am good." Amber told her as she ripped the paper off the arrangements,

"Wow! What a beautiful and unusual arrangement of blue roses. I haven't seen anything like this in my life. You might want to stop over here, before you head into the back and see these," Amber said to her boss as she took the card off and prepared to hand it to her. Alexis stopped what she was doing and let out a quickened breath. Had she heard her correctly?

"*Blue roses*? Did you say blue?" She stuttered as she repeated it herself aloud.

"Yes, here's the card."

Alexis immediately began shaking as she allowed the card to slip from her fingers and drop to the floor.

Amber eyed her boss strangely before she bent to pick up the card. She went to hand it to her again. Alexis took a step back and shook her head hard. She already knew who they were from. *He* was the only person who would ever send her blue roses. She felt like she was in a movie as she slowly turned around and looked at them. They were beautiful, and if it had been for different reasons, she would have marveled at how exquisite they were. There were two shades of blue roses, Peruvian lilies with birds of paradise, and a couple of blue and white carnations with baby's breath throughout. It seemed like such a waste to destroy them, but there was no way she was going to keep them in the studio. Blowing out a hard breath, she gave her attention to Amber, hoping her emotions weren't showing how she truly felt at that moment.

"Please get rid of them!" she spoke in an elevated tone. She heard her own voice begin to shake in unison with her already shaking body.

Amber's head snapped up and her eyes got big, surprised by what was taking place. She pushed her glasses back onto her face and looked over at Alexis, biting her lip in confusion she repeated," Get rid of them?" It was then she noticed how upset her boss was. Immediately without further questioning, she did what was asked, as she stepped back from the arrangement, Amber called out to one of the crew members and had him take it away. Watching Alexis go into her office, she wondered what that was all about, but didn't dare ask. It had been very few times she had ever seen her boss upset, or even emotional. It was clearly too much going on. Amber slowly went back to getting the studio ready for its opening.

Alexis tried to walk into her office on unsteady legs, grabbing onto the doorknob and opening her office door. She couldn't even take the extra steps to her desk. She literally slid onto the couch and sat there. Why was this taking her off her square? She breathed in and out several times in an attempt to gather her thoughts. Why now? Why after all this time was he making himself known? Sean had not bothered her outside of those stupid texts in close to two years. She wasn't going to let him interrupt her life; not this time.

Pulling out her cell phone, she started to dial, but paused; running her thumb over the dial pad she sat there so long the screen went black. Sighing, she went back and forth in her mind, but in the end, she knew she couldn't take any chances, even if she was putting on a good front. She dialed the number slowly, upset that she still knew his number by heart. It was a number she had hoped she would never have to dial again.

✣ 2 ✣

ZAVIER

Zavier placed his phone on the nightstand, throwing the covers off him and pausing before standing up. Smiling to himself he goes over in his mind the significance of what today will be. Stretching he began his regular routine, and he positioned himself on the floor. He counted to himself as he did his push-ups, the sweat pouring off his face onto his floor. His usually clear mind is full of thoughts, mainly of Alexis. He felt his whole body warm with love; he would have never thought he would have a woman like her by his side. His past didn't direct that, he had always gone about his life as a well-oiled machine, and Alexis was his monkey wrench. Zavier was thirty-one years old, but no one ever believed him. He spent his twenties in the service, but it wasn't like any service, he was trained for Special – OPS and it changed him. It changed him in ways no man should ever have had to in the last ten years. He was just crawling out of a dark place in his life when Alexis came into it. Finishing his workout, he stood up and was just about to step into the shower when he heard his phone going off. Looking at the screen, he read the message:

Sergeant: Your presence is being requested, you are to report to the normal location at 0800 hours tomorrow. Do not miss this appointment, like you did the other. Zavier threw the phone on the bed; *not this shit again he thought,* He wasn't going in and he knew that. That's why he tried the scare tactic to get him to come in. He tried to ignore the fact that his special leave was up. He was hoping they would just let him go. Fat chance of that, it wasn't how they operated. No one got out on their own free will. Why all of a sudden was he pressing the issue. He didn't care. He wasn't going back into that life. He liked being a civilian. No make that, he loved being a civilian. He didn't care what was happening; he knew why those last two texts came across; yet he still ignored them from his "former" commander. He went into the bathroom and turned the shower on. Stepping in he let the water wash over him, he wished it could cleanse him from the inside and out. Finishing his shower, he got dressed and headed to the college where he worked. He needed to call his best friend.

3

SEAN

Sean watched Alexis leave from the driver's seat of his Ford Fusion. He had slept in his car; he stretched his legs out as much as he could. It should be bothering him that his long legs felt a little cramped and that the leather was beginning to stick to his back, through his thin shirt, but it didn't, all that mattered to him was one thing—*Alexis*. Sean shifted from side to side to free his body from the shirt some. The car didn't have that new smell anymore, although he purchased it less than two weeks ago. It smelled of stale food and cigarettes, but he didn't care. He had been staking out in front of Alexis' house for nearly three weeks, rarely taking a break. He needed to make sure he knew her comings and goings. It was as if he was in school learning a new subject, so yes, he had to learn her all over again. He enjoyed watching her interact with her neighbors, just as much as he did observing her attentiveness to the children on her block. He could see she was well respected and loved by them all.

He waited until she had driven off, picking up his phone, he scrolled the call log and went straight to her name. He sent her a good morning text like he did every day. Sean wasn't expecting her to respond, although a small part of him hoped she would. It was his hopes that got him here in the first place. On a weird level, it infuriated him that she never responded. Yet, it never made him stop in his efforts.

Alexis told him years ago to leave her alone, but she was his everything. The night she walked past him at the bar with her friends, and he caught a whiff of her Japanese Cherry scent, he was hooked. He had done things to get her attention that he hadn't in a long time, not even to get laid. She affected him to his core, and that was a rarity. So how could she have expected him to simply let that go? He loved her and he needed to make sure she never forgot that he did. Chuckling, he wondered if she had received the flowers he'd sent. He knew she loved blue rose, and today was such a special day in more ways than one. He took a sip of his coffee. Looking into his rearview mirror, he stopped drinking and quickly scooted down in his seat. The car that was coming down the street belonged to Zavier. Yes, he knew his name and he didn't want that boyfriend of hers to see him.

Sean's phone rang and he cursed. His window was down partly and he could have sworn that Zavier heard it as he got out of the car. Her dude scanned the street like he always did, only this time it looked like he was looking right at him. Sean was glad his windows were tinted. He sat up some when he saw Zavier talking to one of Alexis' neighbors. Glancing at the Caller ID screen, the name Ally appeared, causing him to almost drop the phone. Grabbing it tighter before it fell, he swiped the screen and spoke into the phone, hoping his voice didn't sound nervous.

"Hell...hello?" He cleared his throat.

"Mr. Edwards, this is Ally. We have an emergency dispatch. Are you available to take it?" his answering service rep said.

He didn't say anything as he tried to relax, blinking rapidly. She called his name again.

"Ally, I am currently on a job. Please see if Tim can take this one. If he can't, make sure you call me back and let me know," he replied calmly.

"Okay, sir. Thank you."

"You're welcome. Talk to you later." He ended the call. Seeing that name pop up on the screen had thrown him. When he started his IT security company four years ago, he had named it indirectly after

Alexis. No one called her Ally but him. He was disappointed that it wasn't Alexis. At some point he needed to get back to his life and work, but he knew that for now Tim could handle it; he had requested additional jobs due to his wife having their first child. That worked for him perfectly, considering he still had some things he needed to do. Once he accomplished his goal, he would be better. She was all that mattered to him now. He had waited long enough for this moment, and he'd allowed her enough time and space to get over what happened two years ago; she and the police that is. He wanted her! No, he *needed* her at his side forever. He lit a cigarette before he reached for his sandwich without really paying attention to either. He was suddenly caught off guard when his cigarette landed on his pants and then on the seat. Feeling the heat and smelling the burning seat, he quickly bent down, cursing aloud. Shaking his pants leg, he wanted to make sure the cigarette didn't damage his clothes. Out the corner of his eye, he saw the older man with a dog, coming in his direction. He knocked on the window asking if he was okay. Giving the older man a cold and bold look, he quickly retreated from his car, not waiting on an answer. Sean cursed even more as he took particular care not to be seen by any of Alexis' neighbors.

Frustrated, he turned over his engine, put the car in drive, and sped off. As luck would have it, Zavier was heading to his Audi. Sean pretended that he was going to sideswipe Zavier, causing him to hug his car to get out of his way. Zavier's face was twisted with anger as he watched him speed down the street. Laughing, he watched him out of the rearview mirror.

Mission accomplished.

Turning the corner, he parked on the street right behind Alexis' house. He watched Zavier go into his car, and retrieve some things; he then walked back towards her house and headed in through the side door. His hands were full of bags. He couldn't see what was in them, even as he tried to strain his neck. Then he remembered he had a better way to do this.

Pulling a tablet from under his seat, he hit the screen and watched as Zavier unloaded the bags in the kitchen. He must have been planning something special, Sean figured. He spread rose petals on the floor. He wasn't sure why the gesture made him angry. All this effort and for what? Zavier was wasting his time, he thought. Alexis would never be his completely, not as long as he was around. Zavier Wallace was merely a temporary replacement. In only a matter of time, she would be all his. Nothing was going to come between that because Sean Alexander Edwards always got what he wanted!

❦ 4 ❦

ALEXIS

"Hello, may I speak with Detective Spencer, please," she asked in a shaky voice, clenching and unclenching her hands to control the trembling. It wasn't working so she stopped. She stood up and began pacing.

"This is he. How may I help you?"

"Hi, this is Alexis Morgan. You helped me with my stalking case a couple of years ago. You gave me your card after my father was murdered and told me to reach out to you if any signs of Sean returned. Well, he has always texted me even after I changed my number numerous times. But today, at my new studio, I received blue roses from him," she continued to explain as she nervously watched the activity on the street. The detective didn't say anything so she began talking again, but this time she was surprised she sounded almost normal.

"He is the only one who would send me those flowers. I...I didn't know what else to do. This is the first time that he has really made himself known. I wasn't sure how to handle this so I am reaching out to you," she told him as she grabbed the towel that was on her desk, wiping her hands. They felt gritty to her, and she wanted to get the feeling off her hands. It didn't work so she threw the towel, missing the desk.

"Yes. Yes, Ms. Morgan, I remember you and the case well. It has always haunted me that Mr. Edwards was able to walk free on a technicality. Let me make some calls. If it's okay with you, I can send over a couple of officers or put some extra patrol near your business and home. I can meet with you this evening to discuss things in greater detail. Please give me the addresses."

She rattled off her home and studio addresses and thanked him before ending their call. Now, all she wished she could do was get her mind off Sean. She remembered that technicality Detective Spencer had mentioned well. Sean had hired a top-notch lawyer and the legal expert had cleverly convinced the judge that the evidence collected at her father's crime scene was compromised during the chain of custody. The judge agreed, and Sean was released from custody. The memory made her want to throw up. Finding her strength, she went to pick up the towel she had thrown. She grabbed her phone up and dialed Zavier's number. She just needed to hear his voice, but he didn't answer. She figured that he must've been busy. He would be there in the next few hours, so she had to just wait until then. Alexis tried to will the tears away, but she wasn't successful. What was she going to do? Her life was just coming back to order. *Did the man have radar or something?* She thought to herself as she gripped the back of her chair. Leaning over the seat for a moment, she felt her face flush, and the room spin, she gripped the seat tighter, willing herself to just stay calm and in control.

◌⚜◌

AMBER WALKED SOFTLY TO HER BOSS' OFFICE. WHEN SHE SAW HER, she opened her mouth. She quickly replayed what had just happened. All she saw was fear on Alexis' face. Now, Alexis' back was to her, so she didn't see her standing there. She wanted to say something, but at that moment, she didn't know what she could say that would make what had happened to Alexis any better. Instead, Amber tried not to let her worry show on her face. As she tried to shake the feeling off her, she heard the front door open. Slowly, she headed out to greet the news crew that had just walked in. She spoke to them briefly as they began to set up. Once she finished, she headed back to Alexis' office.

Amber walked into her office fully. Clearing her throat, she got Alexis' attention. Alexis stood up straight, and gave her sort of a blank look.

"Alexis, Channel Six just arrived. They are setting up in the lobby. Are you okay?" Amber finally spoke with concern showing on her face still.

"I...I don't know what just happened out there, but you know I am here if you need to talk. You are more than just my boss," Amber told her sincerely

Taking a minute to respond, she quickly got her mind together and forced a smile. "Yes, I know and I appreciate that more than you know. Please let the news crew know I'll be out shortly. I need to refresh my face." Alexis started walking towards her private bathroom. She could feel Amber watching her. Turning around, she smiled again and nodded, assuring her that she was okay. Amber left her in peace. Alexis knew Amber was aware of how dangerous Sean was. They would talk later so they could come up with some security measures for them both in the future. Getting herself together, she applied a fresh coat of lip gloss and eyeliner and then fixed her braids. Taking a calming breath, she looked at her reflection; her eyes were sad, she hoped no one else could sense her inside emotions, so she was going to work on changing that. Right now, Alexis knew the truth, she was terrified and the feeling in the pit of her stomach confirmed it. She wanted to make this day as special as it should be. She recalled one of the last conversations she had with her father. This was his dream for her as much as it was for herself. He was always her number one fan.

She fanned her eyes and tried to keep the tears at bay again. "Damn you, Sean!" she spoke to her reflection. Exhaling deeply, she placed her feelings aside. She couldn't let him win, make that, she wasn't going to let him win and ruin this for her.

Determined, Alexis straightens her clothes, stands straight and wills her excitement of her business opening to the forefront; she headed out to the lobby to greet the reporter, placing Sean Edwards out of her mind at least for the moment.

Greeting the reporters, smiling she sat where they directed her. They fired off questions and she answered with all the passion her dancing brought out in her. Her mood was changing, she was finally feeling like herself. At one point during the interview, she glanced out of the window and noticed the police car. She began to relax even more, thinking that was quick, and silently thanking Detective Spencer for taking this as serious as she did.

Alexis was on her second tour when she had a couple of last minute add-ons. She found herself having to accommodate a woman with her two daughters and a gentleman who was thinking of enrolling his daughter. The gentleman looked familiar, prompting her to ask him if they had met before. "No. I don't think so," he said as he eyed her blankly. Turning, she continued the tour with that feeling in the pit of her stomach again. Alexis, entered in the studio speaking, when it hit her, the eyes! It was him, slowly turning she tried to keep from shaking visibly to the other mothers, when she addressed the parents, he was gone. Excusing herself she went to the desk and called out to Amber, "Did you see that man?"

"Oh yeah, he said he had to leave and walked out. He was acting kind of strange."

"Where is the sign in book?"

"Right here." She told her handing it over to her." Alexis looked down and read the name, and her eyes enlarged as big as saucers. The man had written *Bernard Morgan*.

Bernard Morgan was her father's name. Did he have that much cruelty in his heart? Even with the disguise he wore, it was clear to her that the man was Sean. His eyes always made his appearance known. Her heart sank as she recalled how Sean changed her life on this day, when her father refused to tell Sean where she was, he killed him. The tears welled up in her eyes, and she heard her name being called. Blinking she looked over to Amber. "What's wrong?"

"That man. It was Sean."

"Oh, my goodness, I can't believe he showed up here." Amber told her as the door opened and they both looked up with unexpected eyes.

It was a group of parents and new students. She was having her first class in fifteen minutes. Taking her hand from her fast beating chest, she quickly calmed down, so she wouldn't look as she felt. Smiling she greeted them and had Amber guide them to where they would be. Alexis was getting silently frustrated but then she reminded herself of earlier, Sean wasn't going to win today she went to change and teach her first class.

Watching her students with so much energy, made her feel elated, she was in her world,. It was a space she always wanted to be in , dancing, teaching, she felt the love on this studio floor. When the class was over, and she walked the last parent and child to the door, she locked it. Leaning on it she closed her eyes. She did it. "We did it Amber. Despite the craziness, I have made my parents proud of me."

"Yes, you have, I know they are proud. So am I."

"Are you ready to get out of here and start over tomorrow?"

"Yes I am. Are you waiting on Zavier?"

"Yeah, he should be here in a few minutes, I'm going to go change. You don't have to stay if you don't want." Alexis told her as she reached her office door. Opening the door, the first thing that caught her attention was a single blue rose laying on the top of her couch. Her palms instantly began to sweat, and she began to hyperventilate. Alexis wasn't sure what the sound was that escaped from her mouth, but when she heard Amber's footsteps run up behind her and as she grabbed her hand, out of pure reaction, she yanked her hand away and backed away, shaking her head. Amber's eyes started to tear. She felt helpless in helping her employer and friend as she noticed what caused her cry.

"I can't... I can't breathe," she whispered, trying to reach out for something to hold onto. Zavier walked into the door and went straight to Alexis, he heard her scream as he opened the door, and immediately ran over to both women. She felt Zavier grab her just as the room suddenly began to swirl around her. Then everything went dark.

❧ 5 ❧

DETECTIVE SPENCER

anging up from his call, he turned to his computer and typed
in some numbers, Sean Edwards' smug shot appeared on his
screen. Sean Edwards was one of the coldest killers he had
ever come across. The way he killed that young lady's father was
horrific. No one deserved to die like that he thought. He knocked on
the screen with his knuckle. "I will get you this time, you bastard," he
said speaking to the screen. Pushing his seat back, he stood up. He
needed to get some men out to her place. Calling one of the officers
into his office, he gave him the information and details, and told him
to make sure it was taken care of immediately. He would protect her
better this time than his first attempt. This case always haunted him.
He was up for retirement, but he had always held hope that he could
put this case to rest. Now was his chance;, if nothing else he wanted to
be able to put that young girl's mind at ease. Spencer was just about to
make a call when another officer walked into his office. "Sir? You need
to get down to that studio address you just gave me. We just got a call
and Officer Miles said something just popped off." Without a word,
Spencer grabbed his jacket and high-tailed it out of the Detroit Downtown Precinct. He had a feeling that whatever it was, Sean Edwards

was front and center in this mess. Breathing hard, he raced out of the lot, activating his siren.

6

ZAVIER

Zavier ran over to Alexis, just as she passed out. "What the hell just happened here?" Zavier posed the question to Amber, as he held on to her. "That man...that man was here, and he signed Alexis' father's name in the book, and then he left, and then somehow he left that in her office." Amber told him crying and pointing to the rose that was on her couch.

Looking in the direction she pointed, he frowned and then he picked up Alexis and went over to the other sofa in the reception area. Gently he placed her down and watched her for a few minutes. Standing up, he went over and surveyed the rose and the couch, glancing around the room. Sighing he wasn't sure of the rose significance so he knew he would have to wait. He exited the room and went to where Amber had just backed up to and squeezed her hand. He tried to calm the upset receptionist down. He knew that Amber and Alexis had been friends for a while, back when she was at the community center; she was the only one that she still really talked to from there. Alexis was a loner by nature she had always told him, but he wished she wasn't, so that she could get out and do more than just what she was doing here at her studio. Once he finally had her calm, he had Amber take him to her desk, she showed him the guest book. His whole body tensed. Who was this man, she spoke about, and why would he play such a sick joke on her like that? Zavier knew something bad happened before he came into the picture; *did this have something to do with that?* he thought to himself. Suddenly, the chimes on the door rang. Zavier and Amber both turned when they saw an older man dressed in all black come into the studio. Detective Spencer walked over and introduced himself. Zavier extended his hand to him, as he introduced himself. He then saw Alexis, lying on the sofa. Zavier immediately noticed the expression that crossed his face. It was one of fatherly concern. Zavier knew for sure, there had to be a connection. Zavier never imagined that whatever details she had kept from him would amount to her reaction today; he just didn't give it too much thought. If he did, then it changed the dynamics; he never pried, maybe it was time to change that, but would that mean he would have to talk about his past as well? He thought.

7

SEAN

Sean licked his lips. Alexis was still gorgeous. She had lost a lot of weight and the loc braids she wore now were past her shoulders; the locs were curled and looked exotic which she had curled and pinned back. He had to admit, he liked her new look, however, it did pose a slight problem. He would have to do some alterations; the wedding dress he had bought her probably wouldn't fit.

As he walked behind her and the other women in the group, he kept silent and didn't ask as many questions as they did. His focus was mainly on her; he wasn't paying attention to the tour itself. He watched the way her hips moved and the way she talked, laughed, and easily answered questions throughout. She was good at this and for his own reasons, that made him proud.

He was taking a big chance being there so when she suddenly turned and asked him, had they met before, he got nervous. He decided to make his exit before he wanted to, but he would be back. He still had something to do before he completely left.

.. He wished he could have seen the look on her face once she read what he had written. He had accomplished his first goal; he wanted her to know he was there; he wanted her to hurt, like she had been hurting him over these years by making him have to stay away. He knew she would be upset. Today marked the anniversary of when he took her smug ass father's life. That man thought he was a joke. All he had to do was tell him where Alexis was. Instead, he had mocked him and called him all kinds of names. He'd even had the nerve to spit in his face. He guessed he had the last laugh. He remembered how he had choked the life out of that old man and how he had that shocked look on his face. Her father didn't have the smug expression now did he? He laughed deeply. Carving his daughter's name in his chest was a work of art as he chuckled to himself. Then his finale of spreading her father's blood all over every picture in his home was his final masterpiece. That was the first time he took someone's life. The feeling left him on a complete high. Bringing himself out his thoughts, he drove down the street until he found what he was looking for.

Sean parked his car outside of the bar. Cutting the ignition, he thought of Zavier. Should he take him out the same way as he did Bernard? No, he pondered. Physically shaking his head, he knew Zavier wouldn't be as easy. However, he knew he would find a way to make him fall, just like Bernard. They would all see that Alexis belonged to him. From the moment he heard her laugh, heard her talk, she was all he dreamt about. He could handle all that was going to come up. He had been setting this all up for a while. No one, including the police, that piece of a man, or anyone else was cancelling out what he planned for her. He was going to make sure of that one way or another.

The bar entrance was dark, but he could still see all the advertisings on the wall. The farther he walked inside, the more his eyes adjusted to his surroundings. He headed toward the bar and took a seat in the far corner. Looking around, he was pleased there weren't many patrons. He greeted the bartender and placed his order—a Hennessy with Coke and a splash of lime. He took a long swig of his drink and set the near empty glass on the counter. He pulled out his phone, and scrolled through the pictures he had taken of Alexis this week. Enlarging the picture, he touched her face as if he was really touching her. Hearing a clinking sound, he looked up and noticed the bartender had come back over and placed another drink in front of him. Sean glanced up at him, wondering what he was doing. When the man didn't say anything, he motioned for him. "I didn't order this," Sean said.

"I know. *She* did." The bartender motioned to the woman that sat at the opposite end of the bar. The bartender walked away to service a patron who had just walked in. Sean looked in the woman's direction. She was stunning in her red and she was wearing it well. She nodded and raised her glass in a mock cheers gesture. He imitated her actions, nodding in return. Sean stroked his face and smiled. He never had a problem picking up women. He got mistaken for the actor, D.B. Woodside, all the time. Maybe he could at least get laid, as he did need to quench that electric feeling he had in him from being so close to Alexis. He finished off his beverage, grabbed his new one and headed in her direction.

"Good evening, beautiful. Thank you for the drink."

"You're more than welcome. I'm Monique. This is the first time I've seen you in here." She extended her hand.

"It's nice to meet you Monique. John," he replied, returning the shake. "Yes, I saw this place a couple of times on my way home, so I decided to stop in; long day."

"Oh really? And what do you do? I hope you don't mind my asking." Monique watched him over the rim of her glass as she took a drink. Sean studied her for a moment, while contemplating which story he would tell her.

"Actually, I'm a private investigator for one of the leading law firms in town."

"Ooh...sounds exciting."

"It is. It is. Do you want to get out of here?" he asked, boldly. She smiled in reply.

"You don't waste any time, do you? I like that in a man," she told him, picking up her glass finishing off her drink. She got the bartender's attention so that she could close out her tab.

When she stood up off the stool, she reached his height in her spiked heels. Letting her walk a few steps in front of him, he watched her hips move in her tight dress just like she wanted him too. As she followed him to the hotel a couple blocks away, Sean guessed she was just like the others, and that is how he would treat her, he thought, while he spoke to the hotel clerk about a room. Once they got in the room, Monique wasted no time in locking lips with him. He kissed her hard as he pushed her against the wall. He pulled at her dress until it hit the floor, kicking it out of the way. He pushed her head down until she was on her knees. Monique looked at him, giving a sensual smile as she took the lead. After unbuckling his belt and unzipping his pants, her red-painted lips opened wide to take in his long rod. He fucked her mouth with ease. He was amazed at how well she gave head. Pulling her up right before he was about to come, he pushed her onto the bed. Now it was about to get fun, he thought. Monique laid on the bed spread eagle, waiting on him to get undressed. He watched her as he did so. She beckoned him with her finger. He laughed slightly. *Let the games begin,* he thought, as he started pounding into her.

Later that evening, Sean looked down at Monique's lifeless body. She was a little wilder than he had suspected. They had enjoyed mind-blowing rough sex. Monique didn't mind being spanked hard. She was into pain. He wasn't surprised when she encouraged him to choke her. Sean didn't realize he was gripping her so hard until she began gasping for air and clawing at his hands, but that made it all the more intense for him. He continued to pound into her as she took her last breath; pulling out, he came into his hands as he stood up and headed directly into the bathroom. Sean shook his ejaculation into the toilet and used his elbow to hit the handle to flush. This was the same method he had used for all the women who were his one-night stands. Monique had been his fourth victim. They deserved what they got, he always told himself.

Sean took a quick shower and cleaned up the motel room to get rid of any evidence. They should have known better than to just sleep with any man. His angel wasn't like those women. That's why he loved her so much. Alexis stood out.

He quickly dressed as he gave the room a quick scanning and double checked the bathroom to make sure he hadn't left anything behind. Taking her small purse, he gently closed the door behind him. He gave a fake name to the desk clerk and paid with cash, making sure he didn't face the security camera. Satisfied, he checked his watch. It was almost nine o' clock. Getting in his car, he headed in the direction of Alexis' house, throwing Monique's purse contents out his window as he drove the back street.

Sean cut his lights when he turned onto her street, pulling right into his usual parking spot. He felt giddy. Monique had taken the edge off his high sex drive, but he was still amped up. Grabbing the hand sanitizer from the glove box, he rubbed some on his hands and wrists and was surprised when it burned. He looked down and saw the raw marks Monique had left behind. He hadn't felt it earlier. He cursed, hitting the steering wheel in anger. Then quickly looked around to make sure no one heard him on the quiet night street. He knew he should have gotten rid of the body like he had done the others. Leaving it in the motel room wasn't such a smart idea. His rushing to get back here, had caused this, now that same rushing was going to potentially cost him. Turning the car over, he sat there for a moment in deep agitation, should he go back and dispose of her body? He repeatedly asked himself as he bumped the back of his head a couple of times on his headrest. Damn it! Now he had to make a rash decision. Stay and watch Alexis' house or go back. After all these years, he had just made his second mistake.

𝕤 8 𝕤

ALEXIS

Opening her eyes, she saw Zavier, the detective, and Amber, all looking down at her. She was slightly confused, not recognizing where she was at that moment. Suddenly, she remembered what had happened, and immediately tried to get up.

"Whoa, young lady. Slow it down," Detective Spencer told her as he gently took her by the arm.

Alexis sat back down and put her head in her hands. Zavier kneeled next to her and pulled her into his arms as she cried. After a few minutes, she was able to calm down.

"He's back. He was here in my studio. I... I can't do this again. He killed my father and he's going to kill me. I should have known those dreams meant something. I...I just thought it was because my dad's death anniversary was approaching," Alexis rattled off hysterically to no one in particular.

The detective and another officer stood off to the side, speaking privately with Amber.

"Killed your father? Dreams? What dreams?" Zavier asked.

Realizing her admission, she grew silent. She didn't mean to mention the dreams or the murder; now he was really going to question her.

Zavier sat there and waited on her response. "Alexis?"

"Can we talk about it later?" she murmured, barely. After a few seconds, Zavier nodded. She could tell he was displeased with her response, as he sat in what appeared to be, deep thought. She was glad that he was there in her time of need; it calmed her. He stood up and headed in the direction of the studio's kitchen, returning with a cold bottle of water. He handed it to her and watched her as she took a couple of sips. She sat the bottle down on the floor, trying to avoid Zavier's eyes. She could feel him staring at her. She knew she had hurt his feelings by not disclosing everything about her past to him. Soon after Detective Spencer joined them again.

"Alexis, we have some officers out now looking for Edwards. Your receptionist has filled us in on what happened. We are going to have you on a twenty-four-hour watch, here, and at your home. Maybe it's a good idea to either stay somewhere else or have someone stay with you until we catch up with him."

"Yes, baby, that's a good idea. You know you can always stay with me."

"No. I mean I know I can, but Zav, isn't that giving him the upper hand? I am not going to let him have control over my life again. I am afraid of him, but he doesn't know that." She stood up and took Zavier by the hand. "As long as I have you, I can get through this. Do you mind transitioning to my place instead?"

Zavier hesitated, but after a few seconds, he agreed.

After she finished giving her part of the statement, Alexis was determined not to let her new students down. She got herself together enough to be able to go through with her two evening classes.

Zavier and the detective stayed until she closed up. It was decided that they would bring in undercover officers to screen all visitors, until Sean was caught. The precautionary methods should have put her mind at ease, but it didn't.

After they closed the studio, Alexis and Zavier drove separately to her house to drop her car off, in order to grab some items from his place. She got into his Audi. She was glad he didn't pressure her to talk since the ride was very short. Remaining silent, they walked into his townhouse. Zavier turned to her when he closed the door. She could tell he was going to say something. He gently took her by the arm and led her to the sofa. They both sat down. The pregnant pause was getting to her as she wondered when he was going to say something. Alexis was just about to speak when he finally spoke. She quickly closed her mouth, waiting for what she knew he was about to inquire about.

"Baby, I know you always avoided this conversation and I never pressed it. I know it's hard and I just want to listen. I will understand though if you still feel this may not be a good time to talk, but I have to say this. I am worried about you. So please, don't you think in light of what's happened, it's time to tell me your history with this... Sean?"

Alexis looked at Zavier's expression and knew he was right, she tried to avoid looking at him directly for a few seconds, it made her heart sink. She continued looking down at the floor and not Zavier, he did deserve to know, but talking about him, talking about Sean was not what she wanted to do. She had hoped this would never resurface. She had never understood him. The man had taken so much from her already. Sighing heavily, she sat back on the couch and took in huge breaths, folding her knees on the couch and hugging herself she then began, "Some co-workers and I went out one evening ...celebrating a promotion, I think. I guess he noticed me when we walked through the door. He sent over a round of drinks and joined us a few minutes later. There wasn't an immediate spark for me; in fact, I wasn't interested at all, and I told him that we could just be friends. He didn't like my answer. He started pursuing me heavily anyways; sending flowers daily to my job, my house; neither of which I had given him the addresses to. He would pop up wherever I was, even on dates. That's when I realized he had been following me. My dad begged me to file a protection order against him and when I did he backed off for a short while Then one day, he caught me off guard when I was leaving the community center. When I ignored him, he got violent. He grabbed me and pulled me into his car. I screamed and screamed, hoping someone would hear me..." She stopped as her thoughts invaded her, taking her back to that day as if it was yesterday; the tears collected on her face. Zavier pulled her into his arms, urging her to finish.

"He...he ripped my shirt, snatched up my skirt, and I think he would have tried to rape me. Luckily, someone heard me screaming and came banging on his car window. It scared him enough where he shoved me out of the car and took off. I was so terrified; I took a leave of absence. I wouldn't even leave the house unless someone was with me. My dad convinced me to go live with my aunt for a few weeks so that I could try and get some peace from the ordeal. I wasn't even gone a week when Detective Spencer called and informed me that my father had been murdered. I knew instantly Sean had killed him, it was so horrible, it looked like he tortured my father and it was all because of me. He wouldn't tell Sean where I was." More tears flowed down her face.

Zavier reached over to his coffee table and handed her the box of Kleenex. She blew her nose before she continued. "We never expected he would actually have the nerve to show up at the funeral. He was arrested, but there were issues with the lab. His lawyer got him off on a chain of custody breach. When he walked out of that courtroom a free man, I knew I was next. Weeks went by and I didn't see him, but he always managed to contact me through my phone, no matter how many times I got the number changed. Today was the first time I've seen him since court," she finished quietly, wiping her face.

"What about the dreams you mentioned earlier?" Zavier asked.

She wished he had forgotten about that. She exhaled deeply, giving herself time to collect her thoughts. She proceeded to tell him about the graphic dreams of Sean being in her home when she arrived, and attacking her. She could see the obvious angry all over his face. This was the very reason why she didn't tell him. She grabbed his hand and placed it on her heart.

"Zav, please don't be mad. I just did not think it mattered. They were only dreams."

"Alexis, how can you say they didn't matter? They affected you right?"

She nodded in response.

"Then it affects me too. I just don't want you to dismiss me as if we aren't in this together, okay?" Zavier told her. Alexis opened her mouth to say a rebuttal but it wouldn't come out. She quickly closed her mouth. There wasn't anything she could say to respond to what he said. If nothing else, he had always been by her side. Even though she met him months after her father was murdered, he still held her on those nights when missing both her parents were too much to bear. Touching his face, she leaned into him and just let him hold her for a second. They sat in silence; she could hear and feel the rapid heartbeat of his, as if everything she had just told him was building up in him. When he suddenly got up, she did not flinch, because she expected his anger. She watched him under hooded eyes.

9

ZAVIER

Zavier stood up and walked over to his table. He didn't want Alexis to see him upset. He didn't blame her. He walked back to where she was, kneeling in front of her, needing to have her in his arms. He pulled her to him and held her close. He wasn't prepared for what she told him; didn't even think it would be that bad, but he had needed to know the details so that he could protect her. Zavier held her and told her he would never let Sean harm her again. A few minutes later, he released her slowly and left Alexis in the living room while he went to pack a few of his things.

Closing his dresser drawer, he pulled the ring out of his pocket and opened the box. The five-carat chocolate diamond twinkled against his bedroom light. He snapped it shut. When he walked back into the living room, he stopped in his tracks as he watched her. She looked so vulnerable. He never saw her looking anything but strong even at her own expense. It was one of the reasons why he fell in love with her. Alexis was an only child. She had to carry a lot on her own, he too was an only child, but being a man and being alone was different than it was with her. He couldn't begin to imagine how it felt to keep all that bottled up inside. Alexis was standing in front of his fireplace looking at pictures of them at a couple of fundraisers. He saw her wipe the tears from her face, and it broke him. More than anything in life, he just wanted to take her pain away. Walking up behind her, he wrapped his arms around her waist. She leaned back and closed her eyes.

Zavier wondered if he should hold off on his surprise until Alexis spoke aloud of what was on his mind.

"I sure hope this surprise of yours can top today's drama." She flashed a feeble smile.

"I sure hope it does too," he replied, kissing her forehead. They stood in silence for a little while. Zavier was full of thoughts, as he thought about what he had been hesitating to do since they left the studio. Alexis squeezed his hand bringing him out of his thoughts. He felt reassured that she was worth that risk. His past associates had all agreed to keep their distance from one another unless they were needed, but now with Sean and his antics, Zavier felt the others would be needed. Shaking his head, this was one thing he never thought he would have to do. Standing up, he excused himself again from Alexis. He needed to make the initial contact. His mind quickly thought about his high command and how strained their relationship had been lately. How would he react to this? Zavier needed this; he would deal with the consequences later. He pulled out his briefcase and opened the flap, going to the hidden pocket and retrieved the phone that he kept there; he held it in his hand for a couple of seconds. Taking a deep breath, he sent out the group text: *Blue ghost is in need of help*. Now, all he had to do was wait until they contacted him back so they could all meet. Zavier hoped he was doing the right thing. Entering back into where he left Alexis, he sat next to her, kissing the area near her wrist, he wrapped his arms around her firmly. After a few minutes, he let her go. Zavier walked back to where he left his bag, grabbing it. He held out his hand to Alexis, she took it as he led her out of his townhouse, locking the door behind them. He quickly scanned the parking lot as he helped her in the car, throwing his bag in the back. Alexis fumbled with the radio as he turned down a side street. She didn't say much but hummed to the music. The remainder of the drive to her house was quiet. He continued to struggle with the text he sent out. Although he felt he had no other choice, as he thought about this Sean guy.. Zavier mentally prepared himself for what would transpire from this, because he wasn't sure how effective Detective Spencer would be. Alexis was his life and he would protect her. Even if that meant going back to the old him; a side that Alexis didn't know existed and he wasn't too happy about her possibly finding out about it either, but what other choice did he have? He spent a lot of time focusing on forgetting his old life-style. It was one he was proud of in one breath and then not proud of in the next.

Looking over at her, Zavier wouldn't hesitate to go back to who he was until this Sean character was caught. He knew that deep down; he would do what was needed. But again, could he really go back down that road? He struggled with the possibility. It would alter everything he had become.

❧ 10 ❧

TERRANCE

Terrance heard his special phone beep once. Looking at it as if it was a strange object, he hesitated before picking it up. That phone never went off unless something was wrong. Terrance felt conditioned, he was always trying to put that part of his life away, but he knew he could never do it a hundred percent. Slowing exhaling, he already knew what this meant; someone from the UNIT needed help, he wondered who it was. But before he could even pick it up to check the message, his regular phone started ringing. Bypassing the "other" phone, he hit the screen, answering, "Terrance here," he spoke into the phone.

"Did you just see who sent out an SOS?" the person spoke to him with more concern in his voice than he was ever used to hearing from him. That very concern threw him and it made him wonder even more who it was.

"No. You called before I could, who is it? Reynolds? I heard he was overseas, do I need to be packing a bag?" he asked lightly. Terrance did not seem to be worried about the message, but he could tell something was wrong when the man paused before he said anything. "No, it's not Reynolds," he said finally.

Terrance picked up the phone and checked the message. Reading it, he exclaimed loudly, "Oh shit. I...I wasn't expecting that," he told the caller, clearly shocked that Zavier had sent out the SOS message.

"Yeah, I bet. Have you talked to him today?"

"Now that you mention it, I haven't. I know that Alexis' studio opened today," he told him.

"Well, you know I will get the guys together, but I will follow from the sidelines. He isn't ready for my involvement. I sent him another text to come in and have our meeting. He is still refusing to come in. His ignoring my request isn't going to make this better."

"You know I am staying out of this as much as I can so I am not going to comment on that, but I will be waiting to hear from you, and I will reach out to him and see it I can get some information," he told him before they ended the call.

Terrance and Zavier had grown up together and their mothers were inseparable until something suddenly pulled them apart. Whatever it was, they never let it taint them and their friendship as they went to school together. Then eventually joined the military together. When they had been both assigned to the UNIT together, they were ecstatic. It was a part of the secret service, and they had seen and done things no normal person in life should have to ever endure. It affected Zavier a lot more than him, and when he asked to retire, his request was denied, but they did grant him a five-year leave. Zavier was pissed but he abided by what was given to him. That expired three months ago. Terrance knew he would have to bring up the situation lightly with him about going in, before it got more out of hand. Terrance picked his drink up off the table he had been enjoying before the text and call, and depleted it in on gulp. He got up, holding his cell phone, as he went to pour him another drink with one hand, as he dialed Zavier's number with his free hand. The call went to voicemail. He ended the call without leaving a message. Terrance put the phone down as he contemplated if he should get in his car and head over to Zavier's place. He decided against it immediately. Glancing over to his rack, he spotted one of the first pictures he'd taken with his mother. Picking it up, Terrance examined it; his dark skin was the same as his mother's, he stood at six feet tall, broad shoulders and very muscular. He loved to work out. He was a replica of his mother, from her hazel eyes to her lopsided smile. Placing it down he willed the tears not to start, it shook him when she passed. It was the only time he had shown any sign of weakness and shed tears; she was his everything. When she was hanging onto her life, he asked her a lot of questions; questions he casually throughout his late teens and early twenties, was hoping she would crack, but instead she told him that he would know everything he needed to know when it was time. He just didn't understand what and why was she hanging on to these secrets, even now. He did ask her why she and Aunt Lily, Zavier's mother stopped talking, her facial expression is one he will never forget, she told him, *"Son, sometimes quiet betrayal is just as worse as spoken betrayal."* And with that, she closed her eyes and that was it. He never really understood what she meant, and he never ever shared it with Zavier. Terrance wiped at the lone tear and got himself together. He turned his thoughts back to Zavier. What was going on, he wished he knew. Walking back to where he was sitting before all this happened, he set his glass on the coaster and picked up his remote turning up the volume as he proceeded to watch the Detroit Pistons run up and down the court; it was the best way to clear his mind of his mother, Aunt Lily, and Zavier at the moment.

11

SEAN

Sean rubbed his eyes and stretched his body. He had been sitting in his car without moving for over two hours. So, when he saw the two patrol cars come up the street his eyes got big. Where the hell did they come from? Then he smirked, this must be a precaution from him going to Alexis' studio. Doing his normal, he once again bent down so they wouldn't notice him. Maybe he had made the wrong choice in going to her studio. He watched as they parked on opposite sides of the street. The officers got out of their vehicles and walked the perimeter of Alexis' house. He watched them comb through the grass, obviously looking for evidence of him being there. One of the officers kneeled down, picking up a cigarette butt. He placed it in a bag and handed it to his partner. They continued walking around to the back of the house with the one who found the butt, snapping pictures. After several minutes, they came back around the front and began talking to the neighbors. He continued to watch them, panicking at the thought of being found out. Had any of her neighbors noticed his car, outside of his earlier encounter?

Thinking quickly, Sean made a decision. Maybe it was a good idea for him to just come around at night now, instead of his usual daytime hours for a few days, especially with the happenings from earlier today.

He slowly backed out of the spot he'd been in, pulling into a drive-way, so he could head in the opposite direction, hoping his exit didn't alarm the police. In his haste to get away, Sean didn't see the older man from this morning, pointing in the direction of his vehicle.

✢ 12 ✣

ALEXIS

Alexis handed Zavier her keys before he opened the door and let her walk in first. He was right on her heels like a bodyguard. He quietly closed the door, locking it, and placed her keys in her bowl where she always kept them. It was then that she noticed it was unusually dark. She looked over at Zavier who looked sheepish. He set his bag down in the foyer and took her by the hand.

"Well, this is part of my surprise, are you sure you want to do this?" Suddenly, Alexis felt a little nervous and she could tell he was a little nervous himself.

"Yes, I do," she told him quietly, hoping that she wouldn't regret it; whatever it was.

Zavier took a breath and clapped his hands loudly. In the center of the room, a light came on. It was completely surrounded by rose petals of different colors. The table was set for a candlelit dinner for two. Out of nowhere, a waiter came into view and showed them to the table. They sat down and he poured the wine and began serving them dinner. With a salad being the first course, there was a note attached to the dish. She began to read the poem aloud, but in a low whisper.

"I love you

When I watch you sleep, I want to reach out and touch you
not wanting to disturb the peace I see on your face
when i run my hands over your face, my heart skips a beat
as you awake and smile at me, I see it all I see it all in your eyes
the love we share, the commitment we have, and the desire that is always there
I never thought I would love you the way I do, I think to myself
as our lips touch and I know that I can never get enough
but please don't think this is it
baby we have the best that we haven't even touched yet
running my fingers through your hair, trembling
at the emotion I feel. I place my hand over your heart as you do the same to me
and at this moment I know we have truly become one
you love me, and I love you, and all else seems to disappear
but again, don't even think this is the best that it gets
please believe we have so much more to give
it's about more than the sex, more than the talk
it's about the way our hearts are in sync
the way you finish my sentences
the way I can read your thoughts
and the way I fall repeatedly in love with you each day I love you.

HER EMOTIONS WENT INTO OVERDRIVE. SHE LOOKED OVER AT Zavier. Leaning over some, she touched his face. Once they finished the salad, the waiter served the next dish and another note was attached. Again, she read it in a whisper.

"No words can express the way you move my heart, my spirit, and my soul. No
words can even complete my sentence the way your love does for me
No words can measure the depth of a love that is so strong. No words can
compete with the sun and the moon, as we watched them fall in love. No words
can describe the scenery of watching the bee and the flower mate as, no words, no
words, no words, can ever say I love you with as much emotion as I feel it for
you. No words can take me from my cloud nine. No words can touch me the way

your love embraces me. No words, no words, no words, have ever sounded better than I do."

She cried at its words. She had never seen him be so romantic. He had done some beautiful things, but this was way different. It came out at the perfect time. They got through dinner with as much general conversation as possible. When it was time for dessert, the waiter brought out a dish, but this time there wasn't a note attached. She looked confused. Her hand quickly went to her face when Zavier stood up, lifted his pants leg, and got down on one knee.

"Alexis, from the moment I met you I knew I had found my best friend and the love of my life. Would you please do me the honor of being my soul mate for life. Will you marry me?"

She was so overcome with emotion, she was unable to speak. She had lost both of her parents and they wouldn't be able to share this moment with her. Crying even harder, she managed to nod her head yes, as Zavier placed the beautiful chocolate princess-cut diamond ring on her finger. They never even knew they were being watched through the window.

13

ZAVIER

Zavier wiped her tears from her face, and his own, as he kissed his fiancée. He wasn't even looking for love, but seeing her at that gala had changed all that the moment she smiled.

Once they finished dessert, he paid the food service company. He escorted them out through Alexis' kitchen entrance. He locked up the back and then went back into the living room where Alexis was waiting at him. She was admiring her ring when he sat down next to her. Pulling her close to him, they laid back on the couch. She was still speechless, so he had gotten the reaction he wanted. He liked showing her this side of him. He had been planning this for over a month. Amber had helped him pick out the ring.

"I can't believe you want to marry me," she said, admiring her ring again.

"Why wouldn't I want to marry you? You have been with me when I was down and didn't turn your back on me. That kind of support doesn't go unnoticed, and with your help, I now have my dream job," he told her, kissing her on the side of her hair.

"Well, you made all that easy. But thank you for the compliment."

"No, I should be telling you thank you. Asking you to be my wife was the best way I thought I could do that. I am very blessed to have you in my life."

"I love you, Zav."

"I love you more," he told her as he tipped her chin toward him. She parted her lips, letting him slip his tongue in her mouth. He moaned into her mouth as she sucked lightly on his tongue. He loved that she was such a sensual kisser. It always shook his whole body. He pulled her onto his lap and positioned their bodies as she lay on top of him. They continued kissing. The room was filled with their kissing sounds and light moans. Alexis lifted her body up some so she could begin undressing him.

Unbuttoning his shirt, she ran her fingers over his chest. He felt the electricity of her touch. He grabbed her hand and kissed her fingers. She smiled. Sitting up, she straddled him and he unzipped her dress, pushing her straps down and moving the material of her lacy bra to the side as he circled her nipple with his tongue. She grabbed the back of his head as he bit her flesh lightly. She sucked in her breath.

"Baby, stop teasing me," she whispered seductively.

Zavier laughed as he shifted his weight and took his pants off. Within minutes, they were both fully naked. He reached into his pants pocket and pulled out a condom and sheathed himself. Then he entered her. Alexis never took her eyes off him. That was something else that was always a straight turn on. Leaning down over her, his chest came into contact with her breasts, it was like it was an ignition; he began to stroke her slowly. The way their skin touched was like fire; their lovemaking was always so intense. He never got enough of just touching her. Her scent, which was always some fruity fragrance, and the way she openly expressed her love to him in their lovemaking, turned him on. Not many women were able to do that. That made her even more desirable.

❧ 14 ❧

SEAN

Sean watched them have sex, and it made him feel sick. That should have been him touching her, pleasing her, not *him*. He was losing his cool. He began pacing outside of the window, careful where he was stepping, making sure he couldn't be seen by the officers who were watching her house, not knowing if they would get out and walk around her house. He was furious. He had a mind to go get his gun and kill him right then. Who did he think he was? There was no way he was going to let him marry his Alexis. He needed to get him out of the picture faster than his original plan called for.

After a few more minutes, Sean had seen enough. He was torturing himself unnecessarily he thought, making his way through the yard. He headed back to his car. Although he had planned to be low key that evening and not return, he found himself right back at her house. He just couldn't stay away. The last time he had tried to stay away, she consumed his thoughts. That's why he came back. He felt this time would be just right. She just needed to give him that chance.

Getting in his car, he immediately rolled down his window. He felt hot, like he was suffocating. Sean kept thinking of what he saw through the window. It was causing him to lose perspective, and that was out of his character.

Leaning his head on the rest, he squeezed his eyes shut, forcing the images out of his head. Sean's shrill ringtone cut into the silence of his car, he snatched the phone up. Seeing his daughter's face on the screen, his mood took a quick turn. He smiled before he answered. "Hi, Angel. What are you doing up this late?"

"Daddy, I thought you were going to read to me tonight. You promised!" she whined loudly through the phone.

"I know, baby. Daddy's sorry. My work has me out later than usual. I will make it up to you. Now, where's your mama?" he spoke softly to his daughter.

"You always say that, Daddy. When are you coming home, Daddy?" his daughter questioned him more and Sean felt bad for a quick second. "Soon, baby, soon. Now, put your mother on the phone, princess."

He heard her speaking to her mother in the background. Veronica got on the phone and his tone changed when she started speaking.

"Sean, when are you going to stop disappointing her? She has been up waiting on you for over an hour. This is the third time this week," his wife said. Sean scowled.

"You know I can't control my work schedule. The real question is why you're even allowing her to stay up this late, Veronica?"

"That child's mind is like yours—stubborn."

"Well, you're the mother. You need to start acting like it." He could hear Veronica suck her teeth at his comment. If he thought about it hard enough he could just about imagine her present facial expression.

"Aren't you one to talk? Maybe if you acted more like a father or even a husband for that matter, we wouldn't be having this conversation," she said before he was met with silence.

"Hello, hello?" He pulled the phone from his ear in disbelief. Cocking his head to one side, he was certain that woman had lost her damn mind. Maybe he needed to remind her who's the boss.

Putting his car in drive, he pulled off and started to drive down Alexis' street, but thought better of it. With much reluctance, he headed back to his office to pick up his bag. He had to at least pretend as if he had been doing some actual work before he walked into the door. He was pretty sure his wife was going through his things. He had noticed on more than one occasion that things had been shifted in his workbag. She didn't even hide the fact that she was going through his stuff, but Sean didn't care. All he cared about was getting to Alexis, and to do that he needed to keep up his charade as long as he could. Veronica was very intelligent; she watched his moves closely. She had already accused him of having an affair. She often complained about his traveling and long hours; that's when he decided to bring Tim on. It worked in his favor, shutting her up for the time being. He rented office space right outside of the downtown Detroit area, about thirty minutes from the new house he had just moved his family into. Veronica was livid about the move, but she had reluctantly followed him anyways. She had received a promotion, but she had an hour and a half commute to work each day. He didn't care about that or her nagging. He fell out of love with Veronica the fourth year of their eight-year marriage, and had only stayed with her and tolerated her because of Simone, their seven-year-old daughter. She was all he cared about outside of Alexis.

Sean's mind raced with things he needed to do as he locked his office door, heading toward the stairs, taking them two at a time. He had his plan all set where it would have played out into the late summer, but seeing how things he didn't plan on were taking place, he knew he would have to shake things up now.

Sean opened the stairwell door. Checking his watch, he was glad the gift-shop in the building was twenty-four hours. He headed straight to the area where the flower arrangements were kept. He picked out two huge bouquets. He would be nice this one time. He had the cashier wrap his wife's flowers and put the other arrangement in a vase. Watching her, he wished they had blue roses, but the yellow and peach roses would just have to do last minute.

Paying for his flowers, he noticed a *We Deliver Food* sign on the counter.

"Do you deliver within a ten-mile radius?" he asked the cashier who he knew was new to the job, turn to the delivery driver and repeated his question. The driver nodded without looking up from his paper. Sean smiled; this plan he had just come up with would be easier than he thought. Ordering two celestial sleepy time teas, fruit, and a couple of sandwiches, he filled out two cards; one for the officers' food and the other for Alexis' arrangement. He went and grabbed some sleeping pills out of the aisle as he took both cups and went to the corner. Crushing the pills into the cups, he made sure they dissolved completely before he went back, paid the cashier, and gave the delivery driver a huge tip to make sure their food arrived quickly.

Sitting in the parking lot for several minutes, he tapped the wheel as the music played. He was wasting time to give the delivery guy an opportunity to get there. The card stated it was from Alexis, as a thank you. He suspected they wouldn't question the gesture from her. The dash clock read 10:46. He did a U-turn in the lot and headed back toward Alexis' block. He turned his headlights off as he drove slowly down the street.

The patrol car was sitting exactly where it had been a few hours ago. Sean grinned as he peered over into the patrol car. Both officers were asleep, just like he hoped. He turned his lights back on and turned the corner, parking in the back. Sean walked in his earlier footsteps on the moist grass, careful not to drop the vase of flowers. He balanced them as he pulled his tablet out, punching in a sequence of numbers. Within seconds, he had disarmed the alarm. He used the key he had made, to unlock the back door. He took his shoes off and stepped over the threshold. As quietly as he could he placed the card down first and then the vase of flowers, setting them on the counter so that it would be the first thing they saw.

Walking backwards, the same way he had come in, Sean relocked the door and set the alarm as he slipped his shoes on. When he was safely in his car, he cranked his music up and finally headed in the direction of home.

✲ 15 ✲

ALEXIS

After their lovemaking session, Zavier had carried Alexis upstairs. They spent the rest of the night cuddling and watching movies. She definitely needed the tension reliever. Once morning came, she kissed his cheek and got up. She went into the bathroom and suddenly felt queasy. It was the same eerie feeling in the pit of her stomach again. She wished that it would go away. Splashing some water on her face, she brushed her teeth and rinsed her mouth. She felt a little better. Looking back over at Zavier, she grabbed her robe. She didn't want to alarm him of her gut feeling because right now, she was very happy at that moment and she wanted that feeling to last for as long as she could stretch it. However, she hoped that Detective Spencer would catch Sean fast. He had caused enough havoc in her life.

Alexis busied herself with getting her things ready for her classes that day, packing her gym bag, and placing it by the door. Once she was finished with everything, she walked back to the bed. Sliding into her house shoes, she woke Zavier up. He mumbled something and turned back over. Shaking her head, she exited the room and headed down the stairs, grabbing their wine glasses on the way to the kitchen to make breakfast. Walking through the dining room, she paused. Looking around, she felt like she was being watched. Out of the corner of her eye, she noticed the curtain moving. She exhaled quickly, touching her chest. *Did they leave the window open? Shouldn't it have tripped the alarm?* She wondered, as she walked over to it and saw it was only open a sliver, perhaps not enough to trip the alarm. She closed it shut, locking it securely. Alexis thought back to last night and she could not remember if she or Zavier had opened it. Deciding not to be over paranoid, she headed back toward the kitchen. She gasped, dropping the glasses that she had in her hand when she saw the vase of peach and yellow roses on her kitchen counter. She yelled for Zavier. She heard him stumble and race down the stairs hard. He almost toppled her over as he tried to stop and see what was going on. He held on to her waist to steady them both, but Alexis' screaming made him look up. She was shaking uncontrollably.

"Why won't he just leave me alone? I just want to be happy!" she said, walking out of his hold on her. She never felt so helpless in her entire life. How could Sean want her like this when she didn't want him? Suddenly, she felt bile in her mouth as she ran over to the sink and threw up. She felt so sick to her stomach. He had power over her life and that thought made her throw up even more. Sean was relentless. He wasn't going to stop until she ended up in a crazy ward. Alexis felt Zavier behind her. He was holding her hair while her face was still in the sink. She dry heaved a couple of times, before Zavier reached over her turning on the water and disposal. She could faintly hear him over the running water. He handed her some paper towels to wipe her mouth. When she was done, he carried her to the couch.

Zavier kneeled on the floor in front of her. His helpless expression revealed that he was as perplexed as she was. She didn't have a right to change his life like this. Alexis looked down at the ring he had given her and took it off her finger. She couldn't marry Zavier with Sean still out there. She held it out to him, saying nothing but begging him to take it with her eyes. She couldn't even speak because her emotions were in turmoil. He opened his mouth to say something, but closed it. He diverted his eyes as a mixture of emotions was present on his face. He finally pushed the ring back in her direction as a tear ran down his face. She reached up, and wiped it away. He grabbed her hand tightly, holding it still at his face, speaking softly.

"What? What are you doing?"

"I...I can't marry you. If something happens to you, I don't know...I mean I couldn't bear it."

"Don't do this, Alexis. Please," he pleaded with her.

She didn't utter another word. Instead, she held the ring out for him to take once more. When he wouldn't, she shook her head back and forth.

"I feel like I'll never be happy. *We* will never be happy like this," she said, barely audible. Zavier leaned toward her and put both arms on the couch on the outside of her hips. His face inches from hers.

"Listen, I think I can handle myself. Please don't do this. Without you, nothing else matters," he told her, wrapping the ring in her palm. He held his breath as they both just sat there. Alexis wiped the tears off her face, she tried to stand but could not, because Zavier was in front of her. He hung his head and stood so she could get up.

"I need to brush my teeth again, and then get dressed," she told him. She headed for the stairs. She hoped he wouldn't follow her. She needed a few minutes to herself.

Hitting the light switch in her dressing room, she attempted to look through her clothes. Stopping, she wrapped her arms around her body, holding herself. She stayed that way until the shaking subsided. She wanted to close her eyes but was so terrified that she would see those flowers again. Why couldn't her life be simple? It used to be. She didn't put the ring back on her finger, instead she placed it to her cheek. She wished her parents were alive. She missed them so much at that moment. Sometimes she didn't think anything could take away that pain of not having them with her, now she knew something else rivaled that pain. She just wished she could call her mother, or have her dad tell her what to do about all this; they would have been able to help her. She just prayed.

✣ 16 ✣

ZAVIER

Zavier watched her run up the stairs. He couldn't lose her. Looking into the kitchen, he looked at the roses and got very angry. How in the hell did this man get into the house? He had made sure to lock the doors and windows, including double-checking the alarm. So how in the hell did he manage to pull this off? Grabbing the card, it read, *Congratulations, too bad you won't make it to the altar*.

Furious, Zavier stomped toward the front door. Swinging it open, he stepped outside, crossing the street to the patrol car. The officers saw him coming and looked nervous.

"Does the look on your faces mean what I think it does?" he inquired of the officers.

The young officers looked dumfounded at each other before explaining. "Last night, we got a food delivery from Ms. Alexis. We ate it and the next thing we knew, we were waking up as the sun came up. We are so sorry."

"*Delivery?* Alexis didn't order any food. It seems you two have fallen for one of the oldest tricks in the book. I suggest you call and report this to Detective Spencer before I do!" he commanded, making sure they understood the extent of his anger. He headed back into the house, slamming the door. How could they be so careless? Fuming, he grabbed the flowers and threw them toward the sink. Water, glass, and flowers went everywhere. Zavier hoped his text last night would be answered. He needed to get this Sean situation under control before it caused him to lose the only thing that was important to him outside of his job.

He couldn't have this man controlling their lives. He needed to step up and take care of what the police couldn't. One thing he did know, the house was bugged. He would have it swept before they came back home. It pained him that he didn't think of that before. How else would he have known about her studio opening? He always warned her about leaving her house so open when she went out. She had made light of it. Insisting the neighbors looked out for one another and that she never had a cause to be worried; but as a man, he knew he should have been more persistent in protecting her.

Zavier never wanted Alexis to know what he did before he started working at Sinclair. His military life was a huge deal for him, and so was his mason life. He did things that he had vowed to never repeat. Grabbing the mop and broom, he cleaned up the mess he'd made and the glasses Alexis had broken. Afterwards, he sent a few more texts and then went upstairs to get dressed.

Walking into the room, he saw the engagement ring lying on the dresser. His heart skipped a beat. He wanted to say something but didn't want to push. He dressed in silence, knowing the whole time his heart felt like it was in her hands. His eyes followed Alexis around the room when she exited her dressing room. He proceeded to button his shirt while he watched her place one of her locs out of her face behind her ear. She caught his glance and gave him a weak smile; they both remained in awkward silence. The room lay thick with their emotions, Zavier wanted to cut through it with his reassurance. He wanted her to know everything was going to be okay, but could he? Would he be able to make this Sean guy go away? Contemplating her again, he grabbed his jacket. He could tell she had been crying. He turned his head, so she wouldn't see the start of his own cloudy vision, his tears were brimming. He never wanted to see her in such pain, her anguish broke him; she was the only person who could get him in this state.

Getting himself together, he wiped his face with his shirtsleeve before she could see him, sighing, he saw her walking past him to the bedroom door. She grabbed the ring, placing it back on her finger. She didn't look back at him, but he knew that she knew, he was watching her as she walked downstairs to wait on him. Zavier looked upwards and mouthed *thank you to the one who heard his silent prayer.*

As Zavier followed her to work he could see her looking in her rearview mirror to make sure he was still behind her on the drive. As they were driving, Zavier dialed a number; he waited impatiently as the call rang, three, four times before the caller actually picked up.

"We need to talk."

"Yes, we do. I got your text last night and I tried calling you, but it went straight to voicemail. Did she accept your proposal?" the man asked him in a very dry but straightforward tone.

"What... Uh oh yes, but it is more serious than that. Alexis is being stalked." He wondered how in the hell did he find out he was supposed to be proposing. Then he knew, not much of his life would ever be a secret, until he got his wish.

"What? When did this start?" the man said as he brought him out of his thoughts quickly.

"Apparently before we met. This same man, is the one who killed her father. He is back. I need to get this handled because she is terrified and it's causing her to pull away."

"Okay, send me the information and I will get started. Is this what that SOS was about?" Zavier didn't respond immediately as they came to a red light. He checked his surroundings and then took a huge breath.

"Yes," Zavier finally said. There wasn't any more he wanted to say over the phone.

"When you get the information can you meet me when you get something?" Zavier asked him in monotone. Trying not to let the anxiety rise in his voice, he could hear his friend rattling papers before he finally spoke. "Yeah, I got you like always. Be careful," he told him as they ended the call. Zavier knew that he was taking a risk sending that SOS. He always tried to keep them out of his mix; he didn't want to bring the past to the future. Now he didn't have much choice. He knew Terrance would be concerned about what he did. Knew it was much more he wanted to say to him but knew he wouldn't press until he was ready, but he was thorough if nothing else, so he trusted that he would help him; even with their issues, he still trusted him with his life. The only other person he trusted more was Terrance.

They had just pulled up to Alexis' studio. Zavier waited until Alexis parked before he got out and took the keys from his fiancée's hand. He checked the perimeter and greeted the officer that walked up, just reporting to duty. They spoke in hushed tones because he wanted to make sure last night's incident didn't repeat itself. A moment later, Amber walked up.

Alexis and Amber headed into the studio and began turning on the lights. Zavier's phone rang and he checked the screen. That was fast, he thought to himself as he told her he needed to take the call. Excusing himself, he went into her office. Zavier's friend explained to him the things he had found in and around the house. He told him that he had found two mini microphones throughout the house and six cameras; three on the inside and three on the outside perimeter. He was infuriated. His friend told him he kept them in, but put a tracking device on them, in hopes of getting a location marked for Sean. He also spoke to him about the extra surveillance he felt would be necessary. Zavier listened without interrupting, answering when he needed to. His friend reassured him that from that moment on, they had it under control; giving him the UNION pledge. The feelings over took him as a lump formed in his throat. As he listened to him speak, it brought vivid memories back to him. Zavier nodded into the phone. He understood the silent, but spoken commitment. He hit the red button on the phone to end the call. He went into Alexis' bathroom and wiped the sweat off his forehead and upper lip. Taking this moment, he automatically transitioned his emotions, like he had been trained to do.

Walking over to where the women were standing, still talking, he joined them, letting her know he had to get going. He kissed his fiancée and hugged Amber, whispering a thank you in her ear. She smiled at him, realizing he had completed their plan. He waved to both women, reminding Alexis that he would call her within the hour.

❧ 17 ❧

ALEXIS

Alexis tried to get through the day without thinking about how in the heck Sean had gained entry into her house. She called the alarm company to have them come out and reinstall her security system. As a courtesy, they agreed to do the work for free. Her father had been co-owner for over thirty years. Afterwards, she called the detective, updating him on what had happened this morning. He said he would heighten the patrol. She was surprised she detected a tone of irritation when he spoke. She didn't question him. Maybe he was just busy, she guessed. She thanked him and plodded out of her office to start her classes for the day.

Alexis' mind wasn't entirely on her students today, and it showed when one of her previous students questioned the pivot she had just demonstrated. Giving up, she apologized to them and gave them a free dance. The young girl changed the song on the playlist and the room filled with the new Trey Songz's song. The girls cheered as they hit the open floor and started dancing. She watched them and laughed as they enjoyed the one free day.

On her lunch, Amber brought her some soup. "Don't make me have to force feed you," Amber joked, just before closing Alexis' office door and leaving her alone. Alexis' mind wandered. How could this man, whom she had only met once, but crossed paths with a few times, turn her life completely upside down? She buried her hands in her face.

Pushing the soup away from her, Alexis focused more on clearing her mind. She jumped when her phone pinged. The screen lit up and her eyes widened in disbelief. She immediately got upset. The message read: *I hope you liked your roses. Your response was priceless by the way. Good morning, beautiful.*

Alexis had never replied to any of the texts, but this time, she did. In all caps she wrote: YOU ARE A SICK BASTARD. LEAVE ME ALONE!!!!

Throwing her phone down, she heard the screen crack as it hit the floor. Groaning at her action, she called Amber into her office and instructed her to call and have her phone replaced, her number changed, and blocked, once again. She reminded Amber to give the new number to Zavier and the detective. She had done this over and over, but he still managed to get to her somehow. What made her so special than any other woman that he met? How did she make the cut? Alexis wondered to herself for the umpteenth time. Sean's feelings for her seemed surreal. He didn't even know her as a person. She could still hear his words, the day he attacked her, telling her that he loved her and that she was all he thought about. She tried to be nice to him; to get him to understand the feelings weren't mutual. He didn't hear anything she had said. She was exhausted mentally, and she wanted to be free of this man. She looked at her calendar and decided she needed to focus on work and her upcoming wedding.

✿ 18 ✿

SEAN

L aughing, he set his phone down as he could see her reaction from the coffee shop across the street. Alexis was reacting exactly as he wanted her to. He was getting to her, and she was losing that confidence she always showed him. He watched the officers on patrol as they watched her studio. He had to rethink a lot of things now that she had gotten the police involved. He pulled out his work equipment and made sure that the cell tower he programmed for his phone was still reading correctly. Nodding his head and smiling with the confirmation, he tapped on the tablet screen and then switched over programs so he could check the cameras on the outside perimeter of her house and scan the areas where he had placed them. There was a police car parked on her street. He was glad that he had his disguises of a delivery courier and older man already prepared. Tomorrow night would be the time to put his plan into motion.

He pulled out his notebook and scribbled something in it. He had to write things down now. This was something he never had to do previously. Back when he met Alexis, things weren't this complicated. He should have done all this back then, by now, they would be living happily ever after. He hated to admit it, but for the first time he was

starting to get a little nervous, and being nervous was not in his character. He was starting to get that *need* feeling and it was increasing fast.
His adrenaline was pumping and he needed to get it down. Now would
be the perfect time to see his wife. A thought popped in his head and
rubbing his chin he thought. Why not just kill two birds with one
stone? Smiling, he paid the waitress and left her a good tip.

Getting into his car, he punched in a number and waited until she
answered.

"Hello?" the woman said in a sarcastic tone.

"Now, is that tone any way to greet your husband?"

"It wouldn't be if I had a real husband to talk to." For any other
person, the snide remarks would have caused an argument. For him, it
added to his need and turned him on.

"Are you working from home today?"

"Yes, you know I work from home every Friday," she said, and then
got quiet. She knew what that meant. He was coming home for sex. It
used to be a time when she enjoyed the sex with Sean. It was all she
craved, but ever since she had Simone, he became increasingly rough,
and always wanted her do things that she felt demeaned her. But she
knew what the consequences were if she didn't comply. It was much
worse. If anyone had told her that her husband would be this way, she
would have denied it. Yet she saw him change, she saw the way his
sexual desires had become so nasty and vile. It almost made her want
to throw up just thinking about it, smirking maybe it would be
different this time, she thought as she fidgeted in her chair. At least
that is what she was going to tell herself as she prepared herself for
him. She waited to see if he would say anything else.

"Okay, see you in a few minutes," he told her without any other
explanation. Ending the call, she placed her phone on the table. Saving
her work and then closing her laptop, sighing deeply, she tried not to
let the forming tears wet her papers. Pushing back the chair and
getting up, she went to the cabinet and began to prepare for her
husband. Placing the first items on the counter she finished and then
took the stairs two at a time, heading to their bedroom. She didn't
know how much time she would have before he got there, so she
moved swiftly. As an afterthought, she grabbed up her voice recorder

she used for note taking and set it in the drawer. Hearing the door open, she clicked it on and slightly closed the drawer, rushing to finish before he ascended the stairs. Her heart began racing and for the first time in a long time she began shaking, and it wasn't from the excitement.

Sean drove the route by heart. The block he chose had four houses on it. He liked the secluded feel. He didn't want or need any nosey neighbors all up in his business. Pulling into the driveway, he went in through the garage entrance. He instantly knew she was ready for him like she had been trained to do. The house smelled of lavender candles, which was one of his favorite scents. Walking into the bedroom, his wife was laying on the bed nude, waiting for him. Her body was always a huge turn on for him. When he met her, she was an Alvin Ailey dancer, just like his Alexis used to be. He was always surprised they didn't know each other. The age difference probably had more to do with that than anything else. Veronica was five years his senior. Alexis was four years his junior. He undressed as he crossed the large room. He grabbed her by the hair and roughly turned her around. He entered her without caring if she was ready or not, ignoring her screams of pain. When he got tired of doing her from the back, he pulled out and told her to suck his dick. She complied without a word. She was scared of him, no, make that terrified of him. It didn't matter what he wanted her to do, she would do it. His wrath was much, much, worse.

He pinched her nipples as he thrust hard into her mouth repeatedly. His wife began to gag and he thrust even harder. She tried to pull back, but Sean held her head in place. As she continued to struggle with his large dick in her throat, she couldn't breathe. He saw the tears streaming down her face as her eyes began to roll in the back of her head. He thrust even harder. This was her punishment for badmouthing him and he told her so.

"I guess next time you will think twice about that mouth of yours, but I guess for you, there won't be a next time," he said as he felt his wife go limp with his dick still in her mouth. He came hard and his cum went in her mouth. He let go of her head and watched her lifeless body fall back onto the bed. Picking her up, he kissed his wife a final time before cleaning up his mess from her mouth and body with the Clorox wipes she kept in the bathroom. He stared at her and thought about the life they had shared together. He thought he would feel something, but he didn't. It was like she was one of the other women who he had killed. He was emotionless. Veronica had served her purpose by giving him a child, but as of late, she had gotten to be a hassle he didn't want.

He went into the bathroom to shower. Once he was dressed, he cleaned the bathroom and then went to his daughter's room and packed her a few clothes. He would worry about the rest later. Looking back in at his wife's dead body on the bed, he shook his head. He descended the stairs while making a call to Veronica's mother, telling her that he had to go out of town a few days and that Veronica was sick. He needed her to pick up Simone and care for her until his return. Her mother readily agreed, letting her know he would drop her clothes off later.

He locked the house up, wondering if he should head back to the café. He opted for his office; he needed to be seen in case he needed an alibi for his wife's death. Within minutes, he was walking into the office building and he made sure to make conversation with the guard. After chatting with him for a few minutes, he entered his rented office space, and threw his briefcase on the couch. He went straight to his laptop. He grabbed his cell and saw several texts from Veronica's mother stating that Veronica wasn't answering her phone. Sean thought quickly as the beads of sweat formed on his forehead. He didn't think she would try to call her, even after he told her she was ill. He quickly got his game plan together and sent her a quick reply, reminding her that Veronica wasn't feeling well and that she asked not to be disturbed for the rest of the day. He told her he was sure she would call in the morning. He should have known that her mother would call her; they were close.

For a slight moment, he felt bad about what he had done to her. Veronica was a good mother to their daughter. He hoped that if Simone ever found out it was him that took her mother's life that she would find it in her heart to forgive him. Then he thought, who was he kidding; if it was him, he would never be able to forgive someone for killing his mother. He decided to work in his office the rest of the day. During a call, he was interrupted by a knock on his door. Looking up, he was face to face with Zavier and Detective Spencer. Neither man smiled as he waved them in, both men stood near his desk. Neither man took a seat. After a few minutes, he ended his call. Sean placed his phone on his desk, leaning back into his chair and waited for either one of the two men to speak first. He didn't want them to sense what he was feeling, which was a little bit of nervousness. How did they find him, he wondered? Sean knew his sloppiness was catching up to him

✻ 19 ✻

ZAVIER

Zavier got a call from Spencer. He apologized about the officers' breach that morning, informing him that they had both been suspended. Detective Spencer told him that they had located Sean's work office. He told him he was headed there. Zavier insisted on going with him. Apprehensive at first, Detective Spencer finally agreed.

He reached the location, cutting his engine, and waited. Zavier watched people go in and out of the office. He snapped a few pictures and then attached them in a text. When Detective Spencer pulled up, Zavier got out of his car.

"Zavier, before we walk in here, I need to make sure we are on the same page."

"What do you mean?"

"We are only here to see if we can get him to talk. I would like nothing more than to arrest this sick son of a bitch, but my superiors are asking me to hold off. They don't want any errors this time. So, we have to tread lightly."

"So basically, this is a game," Zavier said, growing agitated.

"I wouldn't say it's a game. That man in there is dangerous. I want you to let me do all the talking." He paused for effect. He wanted to make sure what he was saying was getting through to him. If he went in there in a hotheaded manner, he could spook him, and they wouldn't have anything. "Do I make myself clear?" Detective Spencer put his hand on Zavier's shoulder.

Zavier looked past him and not at him. He prepared himself to see this go the wrong way.

"Crystal. Now, come on, I want to see what this man is about," he said, as he started crossing the street in determination.

Spencer followed and thought that the men may be evenly matched in physical sense, but wanted to try to keep this as civil as he could. They decided to take the stairs to the second floor, instead of the elevator. Walking into his office, Zavier sized Sean up, who was sitting at his desk talking on the phone. He waved them in, but their eye contact never faltered.

❧ 20 ❧

SEAN

Sean cleared his throat, and finally turned his attention from Zavier to the detective. He had to play this as cool as he could. He opened his fridge and pulled out three waters, offering them to his guests. They both declined. He opened one of the bottles and started drinking. Finishing off the bottle, he tried to shoot for the wastebasket and missed. Zavier smirked. Sean leaned forward, finally giving them both his full attention.

"Gentlemen, what can I do for you?" he asked finally, tired of this visit already. Sean was trying his best to keep a straight face and not show that their visit was causing him to be a little unsettled.

Detective Spencer spoke first, making sure he gave Zavier a look to let him lead the conversation.

"Mr. Edwards, I am sure you know that under any other circumstances, I would be placing you in handcuffs, but right now, we are just here to talk. It has been brought to my attention that you are in contact with Alexis again. Is this true?"

"Detective Spencer, I haven't spoken to Alexis in over two years. Is she saying that we did?" he replied, trying to show his innocence.

"She's expressed something like that. Are you texting her daily? Sending her flowers?" He asked more detailed questions and observed

Sean's body language as he waited for his response. He noted that the man's skin color changed, and that his jaw did in fact twitch with the question he had asked.

"Is there a law against me sending her a text? And I sent her flowers to congratulate her on both the studio opening and her engagement," he admitted, making sure not to glance over at Zavier.

"Engagement?" The detective looked over at Zavier who had begun to take small steps toward Sean. Stepping into his pathway, he stopped him from charging in Sean's direction.

"Look man, I am trying to act rational, but you are testing me with your lies. Here's a question for you. If we haven't announced our engagement to anyone yet, how the hell do you even know we are engaged?" he asked, looking from Sean to Spencer to make sure he would make him respond.

"Uh... um... I'm sure I must have heard it somewhere," he said, knowing he had messed up again and told on himself. Abruptly, he stood up, knocking his large chair down in the process. "What's the real reason for you two being here? Do I need to call my attorney?" he yelled, getting angry, more at himself. At that moment he didn't care if his irritation began to show. Suddenly he paused. He gave Zavier a look that spoke volumes. Looking down quickly he began to think how this whole scene was making him react, instead of staying calm as he had talked himself into when they entered his office, he was doing the complete opposite.

"Whoa, calm down there, Edwards. No need to get your feathers ruffled, but he does have a point. How did you know? Even I didn't know that information." Spencer waited for him to answer. Seeing the frustration come across the man's face, his training and experience afforded him the ability to read the signs, and he saw how he could be very capable of killing. After taking a few moments to respond, Detective Spencer was about to speak again when he was interrupted by Zavier, who was now clearly pissed off.

"Leave Alexis alone!" he told Sean through tightly clenched teeth. Sean started to come around from behind his desk as he immediately thought this was going to be a fight he was going to enjoy, but he stopped as he decided to play along with this game he was peeping.

"Or what?" Sean challenged back. He didn't feel that nervousness that he had when they first got there anymore. He still had the upper hand, knowing that they couldn't touch him; not yet anyways. He cut a look at Zavier as he took steps toward his desk.

"Or you may find out what I am capable of!" Zavier spewed at him. The men shouted over Spencer as he made sure both of them stayed in their current spots. Suddenly, Sean gave off a cold laugh and began stroking his chin. He eyeballed both men and wondered what they would do if he pulled the gun out he had strapped under his desk. Then he would really be on the run, he thought. It would change all the plans that he been working on over the last few months. The anger in him intensified as the tension in the room increased. His nostrils flared. If Zavier thought he was going to put fear in him; he was sadly mistaken. Playing his next move, he gave his attention to the detective. "Are you going to stand there and let him threaten me?" he asked the detective in fake disbelief. Spencer laughed lightly.

"Threaten you? All I hear is a civil conversation," he told him very matter-of-factly. Detective Spencer decided it was time to wrap this up. He wanted to be able to keep control of both men and the current conversation, as he knew what was about to happen next.

"Edwards, stop all contact to Alexis, or you will be coming very close to being locked up for violating the PPO against you." Detective Thomas informed him.

"What PPO? I didn't know anything of a PPO!" he shouted.

"Consider yourself served," Zavier said to him as he took an envelope from his pocket, walked closer to his desk, and attempted to hand it to him.

Sean let it fall to the floor. He inhaled and blew out the air hard as the envelope hit his foot. He didn't look up immediately. Instead, he kicked the envelope.

"You know even if you don't touch it, I have a witness that you were served. I think our business here is done," Zavier said as he turned his back on the man with venom in his tone. Sean watched them leave as he bent to place the envelope on his desk, grazing the gun, and again talking himself out of putting a bullet in Zavier at that moment.

"Yo, my man, watch your back and trust me that's not a threat, but a promise." He sneered at Zavier. Stopping in his tracks, Zavier turned around quickly. He and Zavier again glared at one another for a few seconds, but this time they both had death in their eyes.

"I got you," Zavier replied, as he continued to leave the office.

Sean ripped up the order without even reading it. That man didn't know who he was fucking with. It was time to show him. Picking up his chair, he tried to calm himself down. He paced back and forth a couple of times. He grabbed his gun from under his desk, lifted it, and kissed the barrel. He tucked it in his waist. Pulling out his tool bag, he grabbed his lock out slate and a hammer, leaving out the back way in case they were waiting to see if he would react or possibly follow him. He seriously thought they were coming for him about his wife. Since they hadn't, he realized she had not been found yet, but he also had a deep feeling everything was about to change. This wasn't how he had planned this. It had taken him a long time to get where he was now. Alexis' father was the first man to mess up his plans. Now this damn Zavier, they just didn't know who they were messing with. Smiling, he knew he was going to be so happy to show them. He never failed and he damn sure never lost anything and that included Alexis!

✵ 21 ✵

ZAVIER

Zavier huffed as he walked out of Sean's office. He had let him get under his skin. That wasn't in his character; at least his reformed character. The old Zavier would have punched him dead in the mouth, or put two bullets in his head, even with Spencer being there. He and Detective Spencer headed to their cars. Zavier paused as the detective called out to him.

"You may want to take a slight heed to his words. Sean Edwards is a suspected killer. Just watch out," he warned him sternly. Zavier almost laughed out loud at his words, but the detective's serious concerned face stopped him. Quickly deciding to take a different approach he spoke, "I think I can handle myself, besides, I am more than meets the eye," he told him as he smirked. Detective Spencer believed him and nodded. The detective's phone rang, pausing the comment he was about to make. He held a finger up, signaling to give him a second so he could take the call. Zavier continued to walk to his car. Pulling out his own cell phone, he sent a text to Terrance and then went back over the altercation with Sean in his mind. Yes, the man was definitely a loose cannon, but Sean didn't know what he was capable of as well. Zavier was one of the top tactical trainers in his field. He had killed more men than he ever wanted to remember. That was one of the reasons he always tried to keep himself in check. When he went to that edge, it was always hard to come back. That sinister trainer was still a part of him, even as undercover as he kept it. Sean had tested him back there and he almost failed. He needed to do this the right way. No matter how much he wanted to throttle him, he had to show he was a better man. He had just gotten a reply text from Terrance when Spencer walked back toward his car.

"I just received a call on a possible murder. I need to go check this out. I can meet you back at Alexis' studio afterwards."

"Okay, I have something I need to take care of anyways," he told him as they shook hands and Zavier pulled off. He dialed a number.

"Hey, Terrance, I saw your text. Let's meet."

❧ 22 ❧

TERRANCE

Terrance and one of the other operatives walked up to Sean's house with guns drawn. It was his friend with him that had done some true digging and found more out about Sean then they were prepared for. This house was one of them; if they had not come across that marriage license they never would have found this house, especially since it was in the wife's name. It seemed like everything had been since Alexis' father murder. Sean was indeed smart, just not as smart as they were. Terrance nodded and knocked on the door, as both men stood back and ready. No one answered. His partner descended the steps and walked around the house. There were only three houses on the whole block. Within a few minutes the front door opened and his partner stood in the doorway. "Wait til you see this," he told him as he motioned towards the upstairs. Terrance followed him, shaking his head in mild shock as they both saw a woman's body on the bed. Terrance's partner descended the stairs to continue looking around the house, while Terrance pulled a glove out and began opening and closing the bedroom draws looking slightly into them. He was just about to close another one when something caught his eye. Pulling the recorder out of the drawer he noticed it was still on. Clicking the stop button, he re-winded it and hit play, listening he heard a man's voice he assumed to be Sean. After a few more seconds he again stopped the player and laid it in under the woman's body. Making sure he mentioned it as he made a call to the precinct to report the body, he asked for Spencer; he was told he wasn't there, but he reported the body and said he had to be notified, making sure to note the recorder and where he left it. Ending the call, he went downstairs to look for his partner, he found him inside of a secret room that was filled with pictures of Alexis and some of Alexis and Zavier, with Zavier's face been marked up on them all. Taking a few camera shots with his phone, Terrance walked closer to the pictures. Within a few minutes, he was tapped on the back and was handed a bunch of papers and they backtracked leaving the house before the police got there. Shaking hands as they normally did, they went their separate ways and agreed to meet later. Getting into his truck he had just turned the corner when he saw a police car and ambulance in his rearview mirror. Terrance headed in the direction of his superior's office. What they just did would remain a secret, even from Zavier.

Terrance was seated in his commander's office. When he heard the door open, he immediately turned and looked. Seeing him head his way, he stood up and addressed him as he was trained to do. "At ease," he ordered and Terrance took his seat. His commander immediately started the conversation. "I took the information you gave me and did some digging. I am sure Zavier will want to see what I am going to give you, but don't open it. Make sure it stays completely sealed when you give it to him, I should have more information by tomorrow. Oh, and the other meeting has been set, it is for this evening at ten-thirty." Commander Sims told him as he handed over a medium sized sealed envelope to Terrance.

"I understand, and we will be there at ten-thirty. Thank you, sir." Terrance told him. With no further questions he got up and headed towards the exited. He paused when he heard his name called. He saw one of the other officers who was in the UNIT with them, they shook hands. "What's going on? How prepared should I be for tonight?" he asked as they reached the stairwell and began descending the stairs.

"I don't know, I feel like Zavier isn't telling everything, and that there is something wrong with the commander. So, I guess you will know as much as I do tonight." Both men stopped as they reached the bottom, again shaking hands they nodded, opening the door a heading into opposite directions.

23

COMMANDER

The commander watched him leave, sighing very heavily. The information in that package wasn't what Zavier was looking for, but it was what he had been trying to give Zavier for the past few months. Commander looked to his left and looked at his dark chocolate feature in the mirror; his big eyes and thick eyebrows always caught women's attention, along with his baritone voice. It was his downfall at times he thought as he looked away and shifted his attention back to Zavier. He was sure Zavier would be to see him soon after, so he would give him the real information he was able to get on Sean Edwards. It was a little more than what Terrance had come across earlier at his place. Sean Edwards was going to be looked at as one of their biggest enemies. That's the way he needed to be handled. Commander Sims leaned back in his chair and recalled the distress signal from Zavier. He wanted to react as a friend, but knew that wasn't going to happen. Zavier had expressed his mixed feelings towards him, when Commander Sims didn't back him up the way he wanted him to when he requested to retire from the UNIT. Placing his hand on his chest he took a deep breath as the small twinge of pain hit his chest; reaching for his medicine he quickly downed the medicine without any water. Closing his eyes for a few minutes he was hoping the pain wouldn't increase, when it didn't he brought his thoughts back to what was at hand; he had mentally been preparing himself for what was going to happen when Zavier got that information, for a while. Getting up he slowly, he walked over to the cabinet. Opening it, he reached inside and pulled out the two framed pictures he had. One was Zavier's mother and the other was of Terrance's mother. He chided himself for loving both of these women, wishing he could go back in time and make better decisions, but what's done is done. Taking a seat on the edge of his couch he thought back to the night his life erupted, *he had just made it back into town and was heading over to Lily's house; "hey, baby," he told her as she opened the door and he kissed her cheek. She stood back so he could enter, he immediately felt something was wrong. Lily was short and thick, she was top heavy, and he loved women with big breasts, she had freckles on her light brown skin, she always wore her hair in a mushroom. Taking his coat off he waited until she joined him, when she didn't he turned towards Lily, and she was holding a piece of paper. "What's that?"*

"Take it and see," she told him. Retracing his steps, he took the paper from her and opened it. Reading it, his eyes enlarged. Pregnant? She was pregnant... What had he just gotten himself into. Lily wasn't his girlfriend, how did they let this happen. Turning to her, "Are you keeping it?"

"Of course I am."

"Lily..."

"Don't Lily me."

"You know that's not a good decision."

"We haven't been making a good decision these last six months, now you want to have a problem with our choice. You have been in a relationship with my best friend for the last two years. Ain't no turning back now. I am having this baby, and furthermore you can just leave. We are done with this conversation and us for that matter." She told him as she walked over to her front door and held it open for him. Sims looked over at Lily but said nothing, what could he say. Standing straight up he walked back over to the door he had just come into not even ten minutes ago. When he was on the porch he turned back to her. "You know she's pregnant too..." he said watching the expression on her face.

"Yes. That's why I am ending this, even though I fell for you hard, I can't keep this up, we were wrong, now we both have to live with this." Lily told him as she closed the door without saying much else. Sims sighed heavily and

descended the stairs, glancing back up to Lily's house before he pulled off. He knew the things she said were true, he didn't know when he fell for her too, but it happened; but there was no way he was choosing one over the other. He had no plans on ending his relationship with Leslie.

SIMS CLEARED HIS THROAT AND BROUGHT HIS THOUGHTS BACK TO the present. He knew it was time he stopped looking on the inside from the window. He didn't have much time left on this earth and he wanted to make sure all his secrets came out of the dark. Good and bad. Opening his drawer, he pulled out two more additional envelopes. One held pictures of the only two women he had ever loved. The other held his resignation. It may be necessary after his talk with Zavier, so he prepared it ahead of time. Whatever was going to happen, he would deal with it. At least that is what he kept telling himself.

24

TERRANCE

errance looked at the envelope once he got into his truck. What was going on, something was different, it was like he could sense the open tension with his leader, just like he told his partner, he couldn't put his finger on it, but something... was wrong. He had noticed it a few times this month, but always rationalized it to him just being tired. He put his thoughts of his UNIT leader out of his mind. He needed to focus on his best friend, and what he was going through.

Terrance and Zavier had always been closer than the other men in the UNIT, but that was because they grew up together. Their mothers always had them together at one house or the other, they played and acted like brothers. They were only ten days apart in age. They used to tease each other about that. He chuckled now as his memories took over. He wished he knew what changed the two important women in their lives; they lost them both within eighteen months of each other, after that it was just them, and had been that way ever since. Getting his emotions together he fumbled with the radio. Within the next twenty minutes he pulled up to Panera Bread and cut the engine. Looking at his watch, he was ten minutes early. Looking around, he scouted for Zavier's car and wasn't surprised when he saw that he was already there. Grabbing the package, he folded it and placed it in his back pocket. His friend needed him and he would do what he could to help him.

Entering the restaurant, Terrance scanned the room; noticing Zavier, he headed in his direction as he walked to the back of the Panera Bread and sat down across from him. He saw the worried lines on his friend's face. "Man, how are you doing?" They bumped fists. Terrance felt the tension in his best friend's demeanor. He wished he could do something more to help him, thinking of the envelope he had in his back pocket. He started to reach for it but paused when Zavier began talking, he gave him his full attention.

"I am okay. I'm just worried about Alexis. She doesn't deserve this. She has already been through enough."

Terrance didn't immediately reply, because he didn't know a lot about Alexis' past. He knew she had lost both parents but didn't know the cause of either. That was until now. He spoke, trying to keep his voice light, "Right. Right. How is she holding up in all this mess?"

"She has her moments. I just don't understand why the detective could not have just arrested him today when we were in his office. He did kill her father."

"Yes, well, technically yes, but if you saw the file, you would be on this Sean Edwards lawyer's side as well. The police and CSI lab botched that whole thing pretty bad. Edwards may be dangerous, and even a killer, but unless something current surfaces, he is untouchable." Terrance told him, stopping himself from telling him about what they had found earlier. He was about to say something when Zavier's voice nearly shook the Panera Bread.

"This is bullshit!" Zavier yelled, standing and then slamming his fists on the table. Several people turned around and looked at them. Zavier didn't care, he felt Terrance place his hand on his arm, to usher him back into his seat.

"Zavier, calm down! You know you can't let him get you to that point. It's not good for Alexis, and you know it's surely not good for you."

His friend was right, but it didn't change his emotions. He needed to go see his fiancée. He turned to Terrance. His best friend patted his back. He pulled out the envelope that contained the information he was given by their commander. They ordered their lunch and finished their meeting in semi-silence making very little small talk. Terrance offered Zavier some advice before they parted.

"Even though you had to reach backwards for some assistance, don't let this go inward. You almost didn't make it back the last time. Remember that when you feel it taking you over." Terrance reached over and patted his best friend on the shoulder. "Oh, and you really need to reconsider going in for your meeting, it's way overdue. I know that's not something you expected me to say, but as your best friend, I am just saying, it's time! The meeting has been set for tonight at 10:30. I will see you there later," Terrance told him as he prepared to stand up. He saw the look Zavier gave him, as he left him there sitting alone.

✳ 25 ✳

ZAVIER

Zavier sat at the table with his hands pressed against his mouth and pondered on what Terrance just said. He knew he needed to address that issue but it wouldn't be now. Zavier shouldn't be surprised at what he told him; at some point he did expect it. He took several deep breaths to get out of his feelings; it wasn't about him now. It was about Alexis and that psycho maniac Sean. Grabbing his unfinished coffee, he threw it into the trash receptacle on his way to his car.

Once he was seated in his car, Zavier examined the envelope that Terrance handed him with his hands slowly twirling it on his fingers before ripping it open and reading its content. It took him several minutes before he could blink his eyes or shut his mouth as he finally placed it all on his lap. The look of confusion came over his face finally; looking at the pages again he abruptly dropped them as if they were on fire. The papers landed on the floor of the driver's and passenger sides of the car. Zavier was furious; this wasn't what he asked for. Looking down, he stared at his unfamiliar birth record as it looked back at him. The one he had at home in his safe definitely wasn't this one. Seeing his father's name in black and white, he was... he was completely speechless. He started to rip it up but thought better of it. Finally, he reached over and began picking up the rest of the documents; he saw another birth record was included, along with a letter. The other birth record was nearly as shocking as his was. *What the hell is this*, he screamed in his mind as his heart rate increased.

Zavier's eyes scanned both documents side by side. He wondered if they knew. He knew they could not have. Zavier was more than sure they would have never kept this from him, had they known. Finally placing the documents on the passenger seat, he picked up the handwritten letter and read it out loud.

"I know you were looking for something different in this envelope, but it is coming. I took this chance to share what I needed with you, what I have been trying to tell you the past year. You have been ducking and dodging me for so long that I didn't know how else to tell you. I know you are probably wondering why now, and I am sure you are furious at me, and when you are ready, we can talk about this.

Zavier, I know your mind is racing. And to answer the question you are thinking; no Terrance doesn't know. I plan to at least tell him in person, soon. When I gave the information to him I instructed him not to look at its content, and unlike you, or should I say how you used to be; he has always been a dutiful and obedient soldier. I will be waiting on you and until then... your other information will be waiting; I will see you at the meeting tonight, I won't approach you but don't take a long time with this, in this case time isn't on our side."

Zavier's nostrils flared as he attempted and failed to calm himself down. All this time, he had wondered who his father was, and why his mother would never talk about him. Guess he knew why now. *How could Terrance's mother and mine tear their friendship apart over this?* He thought to himself. Picking up his phone, he started dialing the commander's number, but hung up before he could complete it. What would he say? He didn't know, but it probably wouldn't be good. Sighing hard he dropped the phone on the seat and looked at the dash; it was almost seven o' clock and he had not texted Alexis back. Just as he was starting his car, he got a text from one of the officers stationed at her studio. Reading it quickly, he backed out of the parking spot almost hitting another car, as he raced towards Alexis' studio. Calling her phone two times and getting her voicemail, he began to panic as he pressed harder on the gas pedal. He made it there in record time as he berated himself for not answering her or checking on her for the last few hours. He barely placed the car in park; jumping out the car and racing inside.

ALEXIS

lexis managed to get through the day without being on edge. Why did Sean feel torturing her was his right of passage? She deserved to have a normal life; he had already taken so much from her. She had just laid her head down when she heard a knock on the door. Looking up, Amber was standing there looking at her.

"Are you okay?"

"I guess so. What's up?"

"The officer out front said to let you know that it was almost shift change. He wanted to know how much longer we were going to be here."

"Okay, let him know about thirty minutes or so and you're free to go. I can lock up." Amber looked at her as if she said something alien. There was no way she was letting her stay there alone. She was afraid for her boss. She had a weird feeling all day and couldn't shake it. She wanted to tell Alexis, but thought it was better not to mention it. She was already on pins and needles. As Amber was about to walk out the door, she caught a bright glare coming from her hand.

"Um, boss lady, what's that on your hand? Is that what I think it is?" Amber asked her. She felt the excitement bubbling up. She didn't know when Zavier was going to propose. She was honored when he had asked for her help in picking it out.

Alexis looked down at her hand for the first time since that morning. She smiled.

"Yes, Zavier asked me to marry him last night."

"That's wonderful!"

"Yeah, it should be, but with all this going on, I am really thinking of giving him the ring back."

Amber looked at her with large eyes.

"What?! Give it back? Why...why would you do that?"

"I can't get this eerie feeling that Sean is going to try and hurt him because of me. He is dangerous, and he has broken into my house ... he obviously doesn't care who he hurts."

"But, Alexis, Zavier loves you. Don't give that man the satisfaction of knowing he is controlling your thoughts. My momma always used to say, don't ever let someone take joy from you they didn't give you. If you give that ring back, you are giving Sean your joy. Don't give him that power," Amber told her as she held her hand admiring the ring again. She sat beside her.

"Funny. My mom used to say the exact same thing. Thank you for being more than a friend to me." The two women hugged. Standing up, Alexis grabbed her dance clothes. I'm headed to work off some of this tension. You sure you want to hang around here Amber?" Amber smiled and nodded her head. There was no way she was leaving her.

"Um, yes, I am good. If you are here, then I am too. I have some paperwork I can work on," she told her boss, smiling.

"Okay, thank you. I need to get me some thinking time, and I seem to do that best when I am dancing, so I will be in the studio. Come get me if you need me."

"I will, Alexis." Amber walked back to address the officers. She communicated their plans and the officers decided to come inside and watch the perimeter. She served them both freshly brewed coffee and proceeded to do her invoicing. She smiled once she heard the music coming from the studio. She could see Alexis warming up; she loved seeing her dance. It was one of the main reasons she took the job; her love of dance and how beautifully Alexis danced. Alexis used to be her daughter's teacher when she taught at the community center.

She watched her fluid movements until the phone rang. She turned her attention to the caller.

Alexis always danced in dim light; she moved with the music as if she was in tune with each note. Her body reacted to each high note, each low note. She felt like she was a feather as her body glided across her studio floor. When one song ended another one quickly took her head and body into another universe, and she just let it. Alexis danced until her body told her it was time to stop. Hitting the pause button on her music, Alexis dabbed at her face and arms. Poking her head out to the reception area, she called out to Amber, she saw that she was on a call and then gave her attention to one of the officers; informing him she was heading to the back to shower.

Alexis placed her tote bag on the bench, rummaging through it for her shampoo and conditioner. She placed them in the shower stall and turned back to grab her body wash. Her hand grazed her phone. Deciding quickly, she texted Zavier and told him she was leaving in twenty minutes. As she got ready to get in the shower, she heard a noise to her left. "Is anyone in here?" she called out. She didn't get a response. She stood still to see if she heard the sound again. When she didn't, she reached in and turned the water on. She heard the sound again, this time louder. Walking in the opposite direction of where she was, she looked in the other stalls at the end of the changing room. Again, she was met with silence. A wind crossed her back and she turned around quickly. She immediately felt overcome with the feeling that someone was back there with her, as if she was being watched. Alexis quickly walked back to where her bag was. She grabbed it up fast and ran out of there, not even turning the shower off.

Walking over to the security, she pointed in the direction she had just come from.

"There is ... someone back there. I didn't see them, but I felt it," she told him, clearly shaken.

Amber ended her call and came to her boss' aid. Both officers stepped into action, drawing their guns as they went. Amber took

Alexis' hand and made her sit at her desk. They both kept their eyes trained on the changing room.

A few minutes later, the officers returned.

"There wasn't anyone back there, but I did notice a window open. I think it would be a good idea to have the security company come out and place some locks on those windows back there, to be on the safe side, and possibly relock and key the whole place. Amber was about to make the call but one of the officers stopped her, directing her to use his phone.

The security technicians showed up in less than fifteen minutes. They were escorted to the back. The other officer handed her the items she left in the shower stall. Throwing them in her bag, she saw the studio door open. A frantic Zavier rushed in.

"Alexis, why aren't you answering your phone?" He asked her in a panic, relieved to see that she was okay. The officer didn't give much information in his text, except that an incident occurred.

"I'm sorry, Zav, but something happened and I completely forgot I texted you after my first message to you," she told him. She went on to tell him about the shower incident and the open window. Letting him know that the techs were almost finished installing the new locks and adding more cameras. Zavier went to go speak to the owner. Both women sat in silence. All of the men walked up to the front. The room was suddenly full of conversation. They all headed outside, and the studio was secured.

Alexis watched as Zavier shook Aaron Motts' hand. He was the owner of Motts Security. He thanked him for being so readily available for their special needs lately. Smiling over at Alexis, Motts told him that he would always see Alexis as a second daughter, and would be there whenever he was needed. He hugged Alexis and got in his work truck. Alexis grabbed Zavier's hand and he squeezed her hand, somehow that one thing reassured her enough that she told her body to calm down. She made a mental decision right then, she would listen to her heart when it came to marrying Zavier. She wasn't going to let Sean take that from her.

✺ 27 ✺

ZAVIER

Zavier was surprised at how cocky Sean really was. He was glad that he had brought in his old friends. Sean was going to have to be stopped. Zavier knew he could never tell Alexis about the meeting he had with Sean earlier. He wanted to kick himself because he knew his actions were the cause of this. He never wanted to bring further harm to her because he couldn't keep his anger in check.

He thought back to earlier with Spencer. He wondered if his call had anything to do with Sean. He made a mental note to call him, but he would not need to as Spencer pulled up in his car and got out. He addressed the officers, and after being debriefed, he dismissed them for the day. Detective Spencer walked in their direction. He stood there with Zavier and Alexis while they made sure Amber got in her car safely and drove off. She waved as she headed in the direction of home. An officer followed her to ensure her safety, as well as because she had become part of the detail. The couple then turned their attention to Spencer.

"I've got some bad news." Detective Spencer, directed his comment at Zavier. He saw the expression Alexis gave him.

She folded her arms, tilting her head to get the sun out of her eyes.

Zavier knew she felt they weren't telling her things. Trying not to give anything away, he diverted his attention back to the detective, who didn't seem to notice Alexis' actions. Spencer gave a raised eyebrow to Zavier who quickly made a motion to not mention earlier. He caught on. Clearing his throat, he shielded his eyes so he could see them better as he talked.

"Bad news like what?" Alexis finally asked.

"I received a dispatcher call to a murder. Do either of you know a Veronica Edwards?" They both shook their head no, but Zavier guessed it before Spencer confirmed it.

"The body we found is Sean's wife. I can't give you the full details but it was pretty gruesome. We have an APB out now on Edwards. I do believe we got him this time," he said, facing Alexis. "Additional information has surfaced, but I'll have to explain later. Get her home, Zavier. She needs to rest."

Taking Alexis by the hand, Zavier spoke to Spencer. "Thank you. Will do. You will keep us informed right?"

"Yes, I will. I will give either of you a call when I am done." He got back in his car and sped off.

Coming out of her moment of shock, Alexis squeezed Zavier's hand in a vice grip. He winced a little from the pain.

"Did he say *wife*? Sean was married? How? How could he do all of this and be married?" she asked, looking at Zavier.

"Yeah, I would have never guessed that."

"Oh, my goodness, Zavier, doesn't he have a daughter? That's... that's what he said that day. Where is she?" she asked with sadness in her eyes.

Zavier didn't reply because he didn't want to believe he was that much of a monster to harm his child. He convinced her that they needed to go on home and wait for more information. On the drive home, Alexis shared the conversation she had with Sean about his daughter wanting to dance. Suddenly she became quiet and he wished he could read her mind. He hated how this was affecting her. She stared ahead and spoke out loud. "He isn't going to stop, is he? He doesn't seem to care that he is hurting people. How could he take that child's mother from her? Am I the cause of all this? I would never forgive myself if anything happened to you or Amber. You are all I have left." She started rattling off and hysterically crying. Zavier pulled over onto the side of the road. He held her and consoled her as much as he could. The traffic whizzed by them, as it seemed they sat there for a long time. He needed her to be strong, but he knew she had been strong all this time and now that resolve was wavering. She had been through so much this week alone. He wanted to take all her pain away. It took some time, but he managed to get her calm enough so that they could head on home. He pulled back into traffic and got her home safely.

Earlier, Zavier had secretly had the locks changed and switched her keys so she wouldn't know exactly what Sean had been up to outside of the flower deliveries. If she knew she was being watched, it would take away the last bit of security she felt she had. He knew he needed to make her life as normal as possible. He drew her a bath and had dinner delivered while he bathed her. Putting on some soft music they both enjoyed the tranquil moment as much as their minds would allow them. Zavier noticed how Alexis didn't put up a fight. She was too quiet. It worried him, but he wanted her to rest. When the food arrived, he served it to her in bed, again they ate in silence. He handed her a valium so she could rest when she finished her food.

Taking the tray away he made her some tea. When he brought it up to her she had already fallen asleep. Zavier covered her, kissing her cheek. Turning the light off, he pulled the door up as he descended the stairs.

Zavier quietly left the house and headed to his meeting spot. Walking in he noticed everyone was waiting for him. They all stopped talking as soon he entered the room. "Let's make this quick, I can't stay as long as I had planned. Sean Edwards must be watched and stopped before he does anything else to Alexis," he began as he informed his partners of the things that happened today. As he finished, Terrance stood up and took over the conversation. He relayed to the group that he and another partner were the ones who had led the police to the wife and the other information that Spencer mentioned. Terrance additionally shared with them that Sean had killed four other women in three different states, and had gotten away with each murder. They had done some deep investigating into Sean and they were nowhere near finished trying to find out what type of things he was capable of. Zavier sat in silence. His silence just added to the shock he was in from what he had just heard. Why didn't Terrance tell him all this earlier, he wondered. The room filled with small talk as Zavier felt he was being watched. Glancing over to the left he saw their leader watching him from where he has been standing off to the front side. Terrance gave off some directives, as the UNIT members asked questions and then began to file out of the room, each patting Zavier's shoulder or shaking his hand. Soon there was only the three of them in the room. Zavier looked at both men, and wanted to blurt out his thoughts. He didn't want to be unfair to his best friend, so he didn't say anything. Picking up some papers he was handed, he nodded and then got ready to leave. "Soldier, aren't you going to say anything?

"Nah, I am good. Terrance, I will catch up with you in the morning," Zavier said as he didn't look back at either man. Terrance stood there confused and concerned, looking over at the commander. "It's okay, son. I will take care of this. Report to the office tomorrow," he told him as the commander was soon left alone.

ZAVIER DROVE BACK TO ALEXIS IN COMPLETE SILENCE, NO RADIO, NO nothing. His thoughts were everywhere. It was the first time he had noticed some resemblance to Terrance and sadly even himself. Guess he knew why they never got along. Parking and heading in the side door, Zavier went and checked in on Alexis. She was still sleeping, kissing her lightly he headed back downstairs into the kitchen.

He cleaned the kitchen, took his shower, and went to lie next to his future wife. As wired as he was, he couldn't sleep. Turning towards Alexis, he opted to watch her sleep. He would give his life for her. Lightly touching her hair and then her cheek, he watched her breath; he questioned Sean's ability to kill his own wife. What else had Sean done that they hadn't known about? Alexis stirred and moaned in her sleep. He hoped she wasn't having that same dream she had told him about. He lay all the way down, moving closer to her and instantly felt her body heat cover him. Zavier wrapped his arms around her, rocking her. Immediately she settled down, pushing back into his groin. Any other time, the spooning would lead to other things, but now it was a comfort to them both. He closed his eyes and just listened to her breathe. Glancing over to the nightstand and viewing the time on his phone; it was after three in the morning. He needed to try and get some sleep; but he knew he couldn't. The same thought kept running through his mind that Alexis was the best thing that ever happened to him, she was the reason he was becoming a different man. He would be lost without her. She was his breath.

❧ 28 ❦

COMMANDER

Watching both men walk out, the commander stood there for a few before he decided to straighten up before he locked up. He wanted to do more but knew this was all pretty much out of his hands. He wasn't expecting to be accepted with open arms, but he at least wanted a clear conscience, but it was still more to it. How much would take place he didn't even try to imagine. Zavier was already facing issues, and then he decided to do this. He had not realized he had started crying until his vision was blurred, taking his hand, he quickly wiped his eyes and face, looking around as if he wasn't alone. Then it happened, his chest started tightening again. Grabbing the chair, he sat down fumbling in his pocket for his nitroglycerin tablets; he popped the small pill in his mouth feeling the medicine work as it dissolved. After five minutes, he felt better. He got himself together as much as he could and got ready to lock up. His phone beeped as he walked to his car. Getting inside he didn't look at it until he was behind the wheel. *"I have the information you wanted. Call me tomorrow so we can go over it."* the text read. And with that he started his car without responding. He pulled out of the lot and headed home. He would just deal with everything tomorrow. He hoped he would be able to get Zavier and Terrance together. He needed to just get this over with because he didn't know how much more stress his body would be able to handle. As he drove towards his home, he thought about the week both of the women gave birth, and how he had almost messed up both their lives even more...

LESLIE WAS IN LABOR AND HE WAS STANDING BY HER AS SHE DID HER breathing techniques the nurse kept giving her. Within minutes it was time to push. Leslie pushed as the doctor instructed and he just held her hand in awe, one, that she was squeezing his hand so hard and two, that he was really about to become a father. When he saw the baby's head he immediately choked up. Leslie smiled up at him, as the doctor said it was a boy. Even though they weren't together anymore, they did at least get along and that was more than he could say for him and Lily. The nurse handed him the baby, and he looked at him briefly before he placed him in Leslie's arms. He stayed with her a little while before he left for the day. The next day he returned to the hospital, sitting in the room with Leslie and their son, after about an hour he told her he was heading out. Leaving her room he decided last minute to take a detour as he took steps down the hall, he knew Lily was in the same hospital and the same floor. She had been having complications. Leslie told him everything in regards to Lily, he never had to wonder. She didn't know about them, and they had managed to keep it that way. Peeking into her room, he noticed she was asleep. He walked over to her bed as softly as he could, trying not to wake her. He stood there, gazing over her face; she looked beautiful to him, even with the machines hooked up to her. Touching her hair, she moved and then opened her eyes. She frowned when she saw him standing there. "What are you doing in here?" she asked him, trying to sit up. He was just about to respond when they both heard a voice behind them.

"Yeah, what are you doing in here?" Leslie asked him, as she was being wheeled further into the room. Sims couldn't speak as he looked from one woman to the other. Thinking quickly, he told her, "I... I was just checking in on her before I head back to the base. I just wanted to make sure she was doing okay." He told her as he stepped back some. Leslie was right next to the bed now, as she reached for her best friend's hand. Lily took it, and they smiled at one another. Lily spoke, "Congratulations, what did you have?"

"A boy, Terrance Anthony. Now it's your turn."

"I sure hope so, laying in this bed is killing me" the two women chuckled lightly and Sims cleared his throat. Both women looked at him, "I guess I will go, both of you take care. I'll be back later, Leslie." He told them, as he quickly exited the room. He was glad Leslie didn't see what he did. That moment could have been very bad.

SIMS HAD PULLED UP TO HIS HOUSE AND CUT THE ENGINE. HE DIDN'T know when the two had stopped being friends, but he suspected it came out about him cheating with Lily and the boys being brothers. He wasn't allowed to see them and they both really stopped talking to him altogether. That's when he took the assignment overseas and just focused on his career. Although he sent them money for the boys, that's all he did. He didn't press the issue or anything until now.

❧ 29 ❧

SEAN

Sean turned onto his block and quickly hit his brakes when he was greeted with the flock of police cars and the ambulance in front of his house. Backing up slowly, he pulled into the alley and watched them bring his wife's body out on the stretcher. How could his luck be changing like this, he thought? He was always more than careful; throwing his fists on top of the steering wheel the SUV shook. He was just heading home to grab the things he had packed for himself and Simone. The clothes were hidden in the closet. He hoped they didn't find them, there were other things in there he needed. He would just have to come back, he needed his bags. Pulling out he made sure no one was behind him. For the first time, Sean was afraid. Thinking, as he headed to get his daughter. How did they know about his wife? What else did they know? This was all because of that son a bitch, Zavier. He just knew it had to be him.

He eased into the oncoming traffic on Eight Mile and sped straight to his mother-in-law's house before word got back to her. Reaching her house, he immediately grabbed Simone, he told his mother-in law he was late to a meeting and that they had children she could play with. Antoinette, Veronica's mother asked him how Veronica was doing and he didn't respond. She repeated her question and he stared blankly at her.

"Oh um, I gave her some Nyquil before I left this morning. I am sure she will be resting for a while. Thanks for watching my baby. We will see you soon." He hurried the child out the door and into the SUV.

"Daddy, whose truck is this? And is Mommy really okay? Can I go see her?" Simone asked question after question in a small concerned voice as he drove to his hideout. He patted her on the head, in hopes of reassuring her. He didn't know how convincing he would be to her. But he spoke anyway, "It's a rental. And yes, baby, Mommy is resting. She isn't feeling good, so we may need to hold off on seeing her. Can't have you sick too," he lied. When his little girl smiled slightly and then turned her head towards her tablet, he thought he was out of the woods for the moment and that she wouldn't ask him any more questions.

Hitting the buttons on the GPS, the screen lit up, and he scanned the streets looking for police. The bright light brought attention to them in the darkness. He frowned as he began looking at the screen. He needed to find somewhere he could waste some time until he could try and go back to the house. Making a left turn he headed to Simone's favorite place to eat. He asked for them to be seated in the back in the corner. Simone jumped in her seat at her excitement of getting ready to eat her favorites. "Daddy can I order whatever I want?" she asked him and he kept his eyes on the door, not paying any attention to his daughter. She called his name out again, this time he just waved at her saying yes as the waitress appeared at their table. "Are you ready to order?"

"Um yeah, whatever she wants is fine. I'll just have a burger and a glass of water," he told her as Simone rattled off what she wanted. After a few minutes the waitress set their drinks down, and Sean thought of an idea, he hoped it would work, Let me see your cup honey" Sean took her cup and slipped some serum in her cup. It would make her sleepy and he would be able to do some things without her questioning him. They had just about finished their food when Simone's eyes started drooping, he smirked. Glad that it was working, signaling for the waitress he paid the bill as she boxed up their left-overs. Picking his daughter up he headed back to the truck, gently placing her in the backseat and laying her across the seat. It was now fully dark, should he take that chance now? He didn't have much choice he thought as he headed back in the direction of his house, hoping there were no cops still there. Sean crept up the street and cut his lights as he made his way back to the alley. Cutting the engine, he got out, locked the doors and sprinted across the street and down the half block. Shaking his head, he was upset. A police car was sitting in front. Looking around, the one thing he hoped would be an advantage was now a huge disadvantage, he thought as he wondered how he was going to do this. Glad he was dressed in all black he walked towards his garage and then behind it as he made it to the back door, sliding his key in he opened the door as softly as he could. Letting his eyes adjust to the darkness, he headed to the closet. Opening it his mouth flew open when he saw that the suitcases were missing. "Shit!" he whispered loudly. What was he going to do? Snapping his fingers, he remembered he had placed a copy of some of the papers in his office. He was hoping it was still there. Back tracking into his office he went to where his safe was, hitting the number combination the door beeped and he opened it. Pulling the papers out he stuffed them in a folder that was on his desk. Hearing voices he quickly went back towards the back door and slid out, just as he saw flashlights filling the front of his house. Walking quickly, he was able to make it back to his truck without being seen. Starting the engine, he heard Simone move around and he turned to check on her. Pulling the blanket over her more, she shifted and stayed asleep. Sean let out a long drawn out breath, he was getting a little nervous. Once he made it back onto the busy streets, he once again played around with the GPS. Taking the papers out he punched in the address of where they were going to be staying; the huge green lines showed him the original directions that he should have been headed in but now he couldn't chance the freeways. Taking the back roads was going to add two hours to his trip, but it was better than getting caught. Adjusting his route, he quickly finished messing with the system. Placing the wig cap on his head and sunglasses, he hit the turn signal and proceeded to turn onto the street the GPS indicated. After driving for about an hour, his daughter had woken up, and was gazing out the window without saying anything. Sean noticed the change of scenery up ahead. It was all dirt roads for miles that he could see. Turning, he saw his daughter had fallen back asleep. He was thankful; he knew she would be questioning him soon.

The sky was dark, and he could clearly see the stars out his windshield. He had been driving for hours. When the hideout entrance was right in front of him, he slowed and parked in the back where the truck couldn't be easily seen off the road. Sean gathered what little things he had and then went to get Simone. He carried her into the house and into her new temporary room. He paced the floor, running his hands over his face several times. This was not how things were supposed to go. He thought he had at least two more days before Veronica would be found. Thinking back to what had changed over the last day and a half, he knew what it was—Zavier! He was the one person that had been throwing a monkey wrench in his plans, but that was going to stop. He sat in the recliner and thought all night. Tomorrow was going to be a new day, the new day that he would make everything go his way, no matter what it took. Getting up he went up the stairs and into the other room he had prepared, running his hands over the dress and smiling. His whole body shook with excitement and for a brief moment he forgot about all his troubles. Releasing the dress, he stepped back and closed the door. Going back into the living room he clicked on the television and stared blankly at the screen. Sean finally closed his eyes trying to sleep.

❧ 30 ❧

ALEXIS

lexis and Zavier decided to play hooky for the day. She told Amber she had a free day. They spent the morning looking at decorations and things for the wedding. She wanted to go look at dresses, but Zavier said that was something she should do with Amber. His clever way of getting out of having the responsibility she thought, but she let him off the hook. It would be a very small wedding as they both only had one person to stand with the other. It didn't matter. She was just glad she was getting the bride bug. They had set a date for early fall, which didn't leave a lot of time since it was already end of June. They both thought it would be a good distraction for them, mainly her. They decided on a Victorian-style wedding, she was really getting a little excited. It was just a little after four when they left their new wedding planner's office. They didn't want the beautiful time they were having to end. Zavier suggested doing dinner and a movie. Alexis nodded her reply as she held onto his arm. After a small debate they agreed on Wonder Woman. Alexis had even managed to push Sean to the back of her mind. She and Zavier were caught up in themselves and didn't even notice that Sean had been following them most of the day. Alexis was all into the movie. Wonder Woman was a show she and her parents watched together growing up, so it had some sentimental value to her as well as the character being her absolute favorite. She and Zavier cuddled as much as they could during the movie. As they were walking out of the movie Zavier's phone went off, and Alexis noticed that he ignored the call. She knew how hard that was for him, because he always had to take a call. It made her fall more in love with him that he did that for her. She heard Zavier talking as he broke into her thoughts. She smiled up at him giving him her full attention, as he repeated what he said.

"So where do you want to go eat?" Zavier repeated, and Alexis paused their walking as she thought about a place they had not been to.

"Hmmm, how about that new Mediterranean restaurant, Anini's? I hear it is the best," she told him.

"Anini's it is then." He opened the car door for her. "So how did you like the movie?"

"It was absolutely awesome. It gave me a lot of flashbacks, the television time I had with my parents and how we talked about the show after it went off. I miss my parents terribly," she admitted.

"Yes, I know you do. But don't let it get you down; just continue to cherish those memories. The actress who played Wonder Woman made Diana more than a household name tonight, in my book," he told her, keeping up their conversation as he successfully changed her mood. She loved talking about the movie as they continued to talk about it on the drive. Alexis felt safe with Zavier and began to let her guard down a little more. They arrived at the restaurant and were taken to a table immediately even though it was crowded. Picking up the menu she took a look at the décor, the walls were covered in red and gold felt designs. She touched the wall herself, to be sure.

"What do you think?" he asked as he too admired the set up.

"It's gorgeous in here. If the food tastes as good as it looks, maybe we can inquire about our reception being here.". This place was perfect. Zavier ordered their wine and appetizers, while she made her entrée selection.

Zavier's phone rang. He gave a look that she couldn't read as he excused himself from the table to take the call; Alexis noticed that he had a lot of calls lately. Who was he talking to? She only knew of one friend. Maybe it was work related. Since he had been made the Athletic Director, he had way more responsibility. She decided it didn't matter and took the time to people watch; it was early evening and people were walking around the vibrant Downtown Detroit area. Alexis' gaze was caught by an older couple holding hands and laughing across the street. It reminded her of her parents. They were always the type to hold hands, whisper to one another and show open affection around her. Her mother said she wanted her to know what to expect from her husband. It was what she said she deserved. When her mother died of cancer, her dad took over being her everything. He did a great job when he was living she thought, but she knew they were both watching over. The couple looked up at her like they knew she was watching them, and both smiled as they walked on past. She hoped that would be her and Zavier. She wanted that and more.

Looking down at her ring, she twisted it on her finger. She felt good knowing that she hadn't ended her engagement with Zavier. It was her emotions talking, not her heart. Thinking about her conversation with Amber, she knew Amber was right. Ending it with Zavier would have been a huge mistake.

Looking over to where he was talking, he looked up at her, flashed a smile, and put his finger up to let her know that he was wrapping up his conversation. Zavier's smile always made her melt. His dimples were so deep; they gave him a childlike look. It was one of the first things she had noticed about him when they met. His smile literally made her heart skip a beat, and playing with his dimples was an added bonus. She laughed to herself at that. Alexis remembered the first time that she had stuck in her finger in his dimple while he was in midsentence one day. It caught him completely off guard, but he wasn't mad, instead he kissed her hand, she fell more in love with him.

Coming out of her thoughts she smiled back, nodding okay, and then looked back out the window right as another couple left her view. Something caught her peripheral view, and she turned her head slightly to the side, trying to get a better sight of the distraction. Alexis was staring straight into Sean's face. He gave her a wink and blew her a kiss. He smiled so hard she could have sworn he was laughing. Alexis stood up and wanted to call out to Zavier, but didn't want to disrupt the quaint atmosphere. Soon after, Zavier ended his call and turned to head back towards Alexis. Noticing the distraught look on her face, he hurried his steps.

"What's wrong, baby?" he asked, following her gaze to the window.

"Se... Sean was just looking at me," she stuttered. She knew the day had been going a little too perfect. She was stupid enough to believe that he, or something about him, wouldn't surface. Looking out the window in the same direction she had been looking in, he followed her gaze; they both saw nothing. Sean was gone.

"Are you sure? I don't see anyone out there. Maybe it was your imagination." He told her as he began pouring more wine in her glass. Zavier continued their evening; quickly changing the subject as he tried to get Alexis to finish their dinner. He didn't want this completely good evening to go to waste because of that fool. Taking Alexis' hand, he squeezed it. She said nothing, but he was glad that she visibly relaxed under his touch.

Appreciating his efforts, Alexis followed his lead, and pushed the quick episode out of her mind as she shared her thoughts on how she envisioned the reception and she truly started to completely relax again. The food was brought out and they both ate in comfortable silence. She was so full she refused dessert, opting to have it boxed for home. She forced herself forward to keep her attention on Zavier. She managed to keep it up all the way up to the end of the dinner as they waited for the bill. She didn't look out that window again.

Walking back to Zavier's Audi, they walked hand in hand slowly. She had heard there was a carriage ride available downtown now and was hoping to get a glimpse of the driver, so they could ride and she could get a business card. Her hopes were heightened as she heard the sounds of huffs in the distance, pulling Zavier in that direction, so they wouldn't miss it; they saw the horse and carriage coming their way, flagging him down. When he stopped, Zavier helped her into the buggy as they covered up in the warm blanket that was provided. The ride took them through the ever-bustling area of downtown Detroit. Alexis couldn't contain her excitement as she held on to Zavier, as they laughed, hugged and enjoyed the long but short ride. When it was over, they spoke to the carriage owner about their wedding, taking his information; Zavier gave him a tip as Alexis fed his horse and they parted ways. Glancing back for a second, she watched as another couple mounted the carriage to start their ride. Alexis pictured herself riding in it to meet her groom as they again started the walk back towards Zavier's car. The night air was just perfect for late June, intertwining her fingers with Zavier, they talked about the carriage ride. "That was just amazing."

"You know I have to agree with you, I am enjoying the new things they have in Detroit and that just ended our almost perfect night."

"Almost?"

"Yeah, this right here makes it completely perfect." Zavier told her as he stopped and pulled her into his arms, bringing his head down to capture her lips with his. The kiss itself had her shaking in her heels, as his tongue went in and out of her mouth and she sucked his bottom lip, just as they ended the kiss. "Yeah now that was perfect" she told him as they continued to walking again.

Reaching his car finally Zavier opened his back door as he set Alexis' dessert on the floor in the back, when he stood up completely and heard a noise off to the side of him and then a deep voice says, "Yo, my man, didn't I tell you to watch your back?" Turning to the voice, Zavier was surprised by Sean's presence. Alexis yelled out to her fiancé just as she saw what Sean was about to do. Sean quickly stepped back pulling out a gun and aimed in Zavier's direction and firing. Reacting, Zavier pushed Alexis hard to get her out of the way, as two loud shots rang out. The sound was so loud that her screams sounded hollow on the near empty street. Alexis watched as Zavier slumped to the ground. Rushing to his side she bent down to check on him, feeling for a pulse. It was faint, but it was there. She completely forgot that Sean was still there as she tried to reach in her purse for her phone. Shaking, she dropped the phone as she heard Sean's footsteps come near her. Noticing a white cloth in his hand she tried to run but he was on her heels literally. In classic movie style, she tripped. She wasn't used to running in heels. She let out a scream as she hit the ground with a thud. Getting up quickly, Alexis didn't care that she suddenly had a throbbing pain in the back of her head, she was determined to get away from Sean as she tried to kick her shoes off but wasn't fast enough. Sean grabbed her, and she started kicking and fighting. She tried to scream again. She couldn't believe no one was out there to help them. Sean placed his hand over her mouth, she tried to bite his hand, but he was quicker than her, as he muffled her sounds now with the cloth as he put it over her mouth. She felt her eyes closing as she veered her eyes on the motionless body of her fiancé. She felt the tear form on her arm as she completely lost consciousness.

🟊 31 🟊

SEAN

Sean picked up her shoes and hurriedly carried the now knocked out Alexis to his rental car. Looking back, he wanted to make sure there weren't any movements from Zavier since he really couldn't see where he shot him at, and whether both bullets hit him. His concern was to make him useless while he grabbed the love of his life. Killing him would have been a total plus, but he didn't focus on that at that moment. Gently placing her in the car, he had his hands on the back of her skull. He noticed blood on his hands. Checking her head, he lifted her hair softly to see the gash where the blood was continuously flowing from. Damn, she must have hit her head when she fell. He grabbed the cloth from off of the floor and placed it on the spot where she was bleeding. He didn't have time to care for her wound. Making sure she was lying down on the cloth, he jumped in the driver's seat and sped off. Sean continued to look at Alexis through the rearview mirror as he drove out to the house, taking the same route, he had driven yesterday, making sure not to hit too many bumps along the way.

The thought suddenly occurred to him. He had done it! His whole body felt like it was on fire, but he was just completely full on adrenaline. Now there was nothing keeping him from being with her; not

Veronica, not that detective, and especially not that fool, Zavier. Alexis was going to be his wife and they were going to spend the rest of their lives together, no matter what. But if something did happen, he knew one thing for certain- if he couldn't be with Alexis, no other man would. EVER! And he would make sure that happened, even over his dead body.

He continued the three-and-a-half-hour drive in deep thought, realizing things would have to happen quickly. They needed to be out of the state by late tomorrow or early that following morning. He didn't know how much information the police knew, but he was sure they had gotten to Zavier, and since he didn't know if he was dead or alive, he really couldn't decipher how much time he had to do the things he needed. Since they found his suitcase he didn't know if they knew where he was or not. And at this point he couldn't risk a hotel. The pastor would be there to marry them soon, and he would rethink all the next steps that he needed to after she was officially his.

Turning onto the gravel road, he headed toward the house. Parking on the side of the house out of clear view again, Sean gently lifted her out of the car, holding the soaked towel to her head. He opened the door, slowly taking her up to her bedroom, he was trying not to wake her up just yet. He cleaned her wound, and bandaged it. Sean tied her hands and feet gently with the restraints he had placed on her bed rails. Closing the door, he went to go check on Simone. She was still asleep from the sedative he placed in her milk. He went into the kitchen and made a sandwich. His cell phone went off and he hit the ignore button. It was the third time Veronica's mother had called him. Guess she knew her daughter was gone. He still had no feelings on it, so he knew he wouldn't respond. Veronica was just a means to an end. She stopped being the woman he married a long time ago. Biting into his sandwich, he sat in the living room. He wanted to be mad about the way things were going, as this wasn't how he wanted this to go at all. Sean recounted all the things that had led up to this moment. It had been only a week and a half since he sent Alexis those flowers. His plan was supposed to take at least two months. That's why he made all these mistakes. It wasn't like him to have to rush things. Sean knew it wasn't his fault but it is what it is, he thought. He should have done more investing into Alexis' life before he came back. He just didn't think she would be all in love; that was a setback, but oh well, he thought to himself. He then looked upward and knew that no matter what, it would work out, it had to. Alexis had been all he wanted for the past three years and now she was finally going to be his, no matter what he had to do to get her in his arms. In the end, it was damn worth it.

Sean's thoughts went to his daughter. Simone would understand one day; he hoped she would. She was daddy's little girl. He loved his little angel. Now having both of the two most important ladies in his world was all he needed. Smiling, he grabbed the tray he made for his daughter and went to wake her up so she could eat.

32

ZAVIER

Zavier felt the stinging pain in his side and knew that he had been shot. He was smart enough to put on a vest, he didn't share that information with Alexis, but some damage was still done. He quickly scanned his surroundings, looking for Alexis and Sean. Both were gone. He didn't know how long he had been out, so he wasn't aware how much time they had on him. He pounded his fist on the pavement, using up most of the strength he had. He was so pissed off at Sean, but more so at himself. He failed to do the one thing he had promised Alexis he would do—protect her. And now, Sean had kidnapped her, and it was his fault. Zavier winced in pain but he didn't care. He deserved the pain he was feeling. His mind raced as he tried to recall what happened, but only remembering bits and pieces of it. He recalled hearing Sean call his name and seeing the magnum 357 he had fired from. He tried to sit up but was met with more agonizing pain. Pulling out his cell phone, he dialed 911, telling the dispatcher his location as best he could. He asked her to also get in touch with Detective Spencer. Looking over, Zavier happened to catch a glance of something laying a few feet from him; focusing more he saw it was Alexis' phone. Damn now they wouldn't be able to track her whereabouts. The tracker was on there for this very reason. He would make sure they grabbed her phone, whoever came. His strength was weakening. He felt helpless as he tried to keep his eyes open as he slowly typed out a text and hit send, laying his phone on the ground next to him. He waited. Closing his eyes, he heard the sirens and was glad they had finally made it. He could hear people talking, although it was muffled and seemed far away to him. He heard footsteps and that is the last thing he heard before the pain really took over. Laying his head flat on the ground, he felt the paramedics touch his body.

"Sir...sir can you hear me?" one of the paramedics asked him. All he could do was blink his eyes.

"Don't move, we are going to stabilize you." Zavier closed his eyes and he saw Alexis' face. He began to pray. He wanted Alexis found before Sean did something to her. He felt his body being lifted off the ground as he was placed in the ambulance. Within minutes he felt one of the paramedics injecting him with something, they continued asking him questions as he nodded his responses, until he could not do anything else. "Grab... Grab her phone please, please don't leave without it," he said to the medic as he grabbed his shirt. The medic turned around and looked in the direction he had motioned to, seeing it he picked it up, setting it on the gurney as he climbed into the back of the ambulance with him.

Zavier opened his eyes and saw his best friend Terrance sitting next to the bed. He tried lifting his head but the pain hit him. He figured his best friend would be the one sitting next to him waiting.

"Alexis?" he whispered. His friend stood up. Coming over to the bed, Terrance gave him a concerned look. He was lucky to be alive, that bulletproof vest had saved his life.

"I'm so glad you're awake. The bullet deeply grazed you, but because of your lifer, no organs were hit. You just lost a lot of blood and got some stitches to close the open skin," his best friend rattled off.

Zavier didn't care about being shot, he cared about his fiancée. He tried to speak and his mouth was very dry. He motioned for the water he saw sitting on the table next to his bed. Terrance reached over and handed it to him. He began taking sips. He stopped and started again. After a few more sips, he was sure he would be able to talk better. He looked at his friend whose expression he couldn't read, and that worried him. Was she dead? His heart started racing, and a tear left his eye. Wiping it away quickly, he found the courage to ask.

"Terrance, please tell me. Did you...did you find her?" he asked with hopeful eyes but deep down he knew the answer, she wasn't in his room, that said it all. Just as Terrance was about to respond, Detective Spencer walked in.

"Zavier, glad to see you're woke. Don't worry. We have every man out there looking for her. I am glad you heeded my warning and had that jacket on. I am going on air in fifteen minutes. I will make sure she knows you're safe, and that we are looking for her. If she is out there and can see the broadcast she will know what she needs to know. Get some rest. We will find her. He won't get far."

"Wait. Do you have it?

"Have it? Have what?"

"I had them grab her phone, do you, have it?"

"Yes, I have it. But will it help?"

"Fingerprints... I don't know," he said aspirated. The detective patted his shoulder, nodding his understanding and walked out of the hospital room just as quickly as he had breezed in a few moments before. Zavier let out a hard breath, looking over to Terrance they shared a look, and Terrance nodded.

Terrance dialed a number and spoke softly into the phone. Terrance knew what to do, they shared a lot, he was more than his partner in combat. He knew his friend would make things happen that the police never could. Their agenda was to make sure that Sean Edwards never hurt another person, by any means needed. He closed his eyes as he felt the pain medicine take effect. He wished his best friend had left him alone. He didn't want him to see him emotional, but he wanted her safe. He needed her to be with him, and more so, he needed to be out of this hospital bed looking for her. He never felt a pain so deep and it had nothing to do with being shot. Dropping his head back on the pillow he stared at the ceiling. His mind was running rampant. The door opened and the nurse came in checking his vitals and looking at the machine that was hooked up to him. He didn't say a word, just nodded with her few questions, as she pumped him with pain meds, he felt them take over his body as his eyes felt heavy.

33

TERRANCE

errance watched the nurse do her job; when she gave him the meds he knew he would have some silence soon. He glanced at his watch as he pulled his chair off to the side and sat down. He saw Zavier's eyes closing. He glanced at the television absentmindedly until he heard a knock on the hospital room door. Turning as it opened he stood up to greet his commander. "Thank you for coming, sir."

"Of course, of course. How is he doing?"

"He is doing okay. He is hurting more on the inside than out. I have already put our other plan in progress. I just hope it goes as we planned."

"I'm sure it will. We have our best man on the job. That is outside of you and Zavier."

"Thank you for the compliment, um I wanted to ask you something."

"Ask me something. Okay go head." Commander Sims told him as he looked from Terrance and then over to Zavier, whose eyes were still closed, before he gave him his full attention.

"Is everything okay with you? You seem a little different lately. I know things still aren't right between you and Zavier." Terrance asked him as he stood in silence and waited for his reply. Commander Sims didn't say anything right away as he stroked his chin. "Son, no things aren't well with me...my health has been failing, so I have decided to step down and I wanted to tell Zavier before I told the rest of you. But you are right he still won't talk to me. I was hoping me coming here would change that."

"Is there anything I can do to help?"

"No. No. You have already helped more than you know. For the moment this is between us." He said. Terrance was confused by his comment and he was about to say something when they both heard Zavier moan. Commander Sims walked closer to the bed and watched him. This confused Terrance even more. He had never ever seen his superior with the concerned look he had on his face for Zavier, for him or any other of the other men in the unit. Zavier opened his eyes and his mouth quickly turned to a frown. Turning to Terrance he spoke, "Give us a minute, sergeant." Terrance nodded, and walked out of the room. Zavier looked at Commander Sims with slit eyes. "Why are you here?"

❧ 34 ❧

ALEXIS

lexis opened her eyes but felt like she had been hit by a Mack truck. She tried to lift her hands but couldn't Wincing from the pain, she tried to look around the dark room. Squinting several times, she was able to see things come into view. She wished she knew where she was. She could tell she was in a room of some kind. Alexis knew that she was on a bed. She noticed for the first time that her hands and feet were restrained. She tried to release her hands, but was met with pain. Sean had knocked her out and she wasn't even sure how long she had been there, as she had gone in and out of consciousness a few times. She jumped at the sound of keys jingling. They didn't sound as close, but she felt he was. She closed her eyes, trying to calm herself so that she could pretend that she was asleep. Her heart thumped loudly in her chest. The door creaked when it opened. Even through closed lids, she could see the light that poured into the room.

His footsteps grew closer; her natural instinct was to flinch. She felt him kneel over her, his hot breath moving her hair. When he touched her, it took so much out of her not to throw up. His hands on her literally made her sick. Sean touched her hair, checking her injury. Once he was satisfied with whatever he was doing, he gently began jarring her. She made a low moan as if she was slowly awakening. She saw it in a movie once and didn't know why it came to her to do it, but it worked.

"Alexis, my dear, wake up. I want you to see your new place. I did this room just like your room at your house." She opened her eyes, fluttering her eyelids from the light. She refused to look at him once her eyes adjusted she didn't respond. She closed her eyes back and peered at him through slits. Once she finished getting herself together more, she still refused to say anything to Sean. Observing the room, she saw a similar blue rose bouquet like that one he had delivered at her studio. Her eyes traveled upwards at his size. It seemed like he was double his original size. Sean finished opening the curtains. She turned her head. The light still hurt her eyes. She needed time to adjust to the change from darkness to all this bright light coming from two angles. She scooted her body in an effort to get some comfort, but she moved too fast and the back of her head began to pound. Finally, she was able to look around and see that she was in a canopy bed. There was a dresser, TV, and a table in the room. It was very similar to her current bedroom. The furnishings, down to her bedspread, were exactly the same. It hurt her heart to see how much creativity and commitment he had put into all this. As he sat on the bed she noticed a wedding dress hanging on a hook on the door. She gasped out loud. Sean heard the sound she made and smiled at her. She couldn't believe her eyes. Did he think she was going to wear that?

"Do you like your wedding dress? I know that you are going to make a beautiful bride and me a great wife. I can't wait to begin our life together. You have made me wait a very long time for this. Now that your *supposed* fiancé is out of the way, we can make this happen."

Alexis' eyes opened wildly, recalling the gun firing at Zavier. Was he dead? All this was her fault; from her father being dead to him hurting or even killing Zavier too. Alexis' eyes filled instantly with tears, they spilled onto her chest and in the right ear. Her ear clogged up, like she had been underwater. Shifting her head, she felt the tears drain from her ear as it unclogged itself. She couldn't remember what happened, but what did it matter now. If he was dead, she wanted to be dead too. She balled her tied hand and tried to feel for her ring. That would make her feel a connection to him. The ring was gone. Sean must have taken it off her finger, he held up her ring. "Is this what you're feeling for? I have to admit he does have good taste. I am sure we will get a few dollars for it," he told her as he dropped it on the desk. Sean saw her tears and he became irate. For no reason at all, he tightened her restraints. She cried out slightly from the unexpected pain.

"Sean, please, you're hurting me!" she told him, feeling as if she was living out her nightmare she had been having over and over again.

"Do you think I wanted to do this? I came at you honestly and you rejected me like a bad piece of meat. You did this!"

"I didn't do this? *You* did this! I told you I wasn't interested. What made me so much different than anyone else? I guess it doesn't even matter that you had a wife that I never knew about until you killed her!"

"Killed her... How did you find that out? Humph, I guess it doesn't even matter now or that I never mentioned her. Now that you mention that, it seems fitting that I fell for her, just like you. Only difference is, she got with the program. I am sure you will too. She was a dancer too, just like you." Sean wanted to see her hurt, like he was, just from the comments she made. He leaned in close to her face. "For the record, your man is probably dead," he spewed toward her, taking pleasure in seeing her wince at his words. It didn't matter that he wasn't for sure, if he was alive or not. He wanted her to think he was. Sean got up, picking up the clean gauze for her wound he had thrown on the floor earlier. Turning, he reached for the doorknob, stopping in his tracks at her words.

"Sean, why? Why would you take away everything I love if you claim to love me the way you say you do?"

Sean didn't even look at her. He continued out the door, locking it behind him. A few seconds later, he reopened it. He placed his free hand on his side. "Remember this clearly. I told you before, if I can't be with you, no one else will. I promise you I will keep my word on that. You may have thought you loved him, but he can't hold a candle to the things I can do for you." He closed the door behind him again, locking it.

Alexis tried to reason all this in her head. But it hurt to even think.

She wanted to sleep, maybe that would make whatever he was going to do to her come closer. She wanted out of this room and out of this house. She squirmed and the ties bit into her skin even more. She gave up because she was getting tired. She accepted that she wasn't going to get out of there without help. "Breakfast will be ready soon." Sean's voice boomed inside the room. It was the first time she noticed the baby monitor on her nightstand. There went her opportunity to try to escape.

Alexis let out a loud frustrated wail and kicked her legs. The leg restraints cut into her skin. The pain followed by the blood was immediate. She watched as it ran down her ankles. She cried for several more minutes until she had a hard time breathing. Her name being said on the TV caught her attention. Her picture was plastered across the screen, along with Detective Spencer, who was notifying the public on her abduction. She wished he had special powers. As the detective continued with his speech, she closed her eyes, willing him her location. She wished it were truly that simple. Was he going to mention Zavier? She had to know if he was all right. He gave a brief description of Sean's car. She couldn't remember what kind it was. However, she did know it wasn't his original Fusion. It smelled different. Her head snapped back up when she finally heard what she had been waiting on.

"Alexis, if you're out there, we are looking for you! Your fiancé is in good condition and will pull through," he said to the camera. With his words, she exhaled all the air she was holding. Knowing that Zavier was alive, seemingly gave her strength and clarity. She took a couple of deep breaths and began psyching herself out; something she had learned from her dad. She scanned the room, wondering how she would escape after she unhooked herself. She thought of several movies she had watched, recalling an antic from one of them that she could use to get her out of this situation.

☙ 35 ❧

SEAN

Sean stood on the outside of her door fuming, maybe this man was a little more than he bargained for, he was hoping they would have been gone before they found Veronica's body. Hunching his shoulders, he stood upright and headed downstairs. Hearing the voices on the television he looked over and scowled. So, the bastard was still alive. It didn't matter, they wouldn't find them. He picked up his cell phone and made a call to Tim.

"Man, what's going on? The police just left my house asking all kinds of questions!" Tim's voice was escalated; he could tell he was still nervous. He waited a few moments to let him calm down before he spoke. "What did you tell them?" He asked. He never told Tim any of his plans, but he still wanted to know what he had revealed. He would have to make it quick, knowing his phone may be currently tapped.

"What was I supposed to tell them? I don't know anything. And that's what I told them. I don't understand what you're doing, but don't call me man. I don't need this heat on me and my family. I've been nothing but loyal to you these past few years, but your dirty hands are yours to clean!"

"I understand and I am sorry. I just wanted to tell you that I left all the tools I borrowed from you, in the office. I didn't want them to sit there. Take care man," he told Tim, hoping that he understood and remembered his clue word. They had always talked about having code words and borrowed tools, meaning Sean had left him a stash of money. He didn't want him to pay for his actions in any way. He was right, he had always been loyal to him, and that $100,000 would come in handy until he found more work. The police that were listening in probably were headed back to his office to see what tools he was talking about, but that wasn't the office he was referring to. Sean was happy he had done one thing right; now at least that wouldn't be on the little conscience he did have.

Sean went back to what he was doing before more of the news report came on. Finishing the touches on the two trays, he smiled the first time that morning. This time tomorrow, Alexis would be his wife, and all three of them would be on their way out of the state, and eventually out of the country.

Looking at his watch, he had six hours before the pastor arrived. He went to wake up his little princess so he could feed her before he got her dressed for the wedding. Walking into her room, he was surprised to see his daughter gone, but then he heard voices coming from upstairs and hurried into that direction. He silently chided himself for leaving the keys in the door. Slowly, he walked up the stairs so that he could hear the conversation between the two.

"Why are you crying?" Simone asked Alexis as she walked farther into the room. She used the tissue in her hand and dabbed Alexis' eyes. Alexis looked at the little girl who favored her father greatly, she was brown skin with beautiful brown eyes with green specs, she had long hair light brown which were in ponytails.

"I'm sorry, sweetie. I'm just a little upset, but I don't want to upset you. What's your name?"

"Simone Annette Edwards," his daughter replied. She had given Alexis her full name, exactly how Veronica had taught her.

"Wow, that's a beautiful name for a beautiful girl. Can I ask you for a favor?"

"Thank you. Um, yes, you can," Simone responded shyly. Alexis took this moment to talk to Simone briefly and they shared a small conversation, when they were done she asked her softly, "How old are you?"

But before his daughter could respond, Sean interrupted their conversation, as they both heard the footsteps and Sean opened the door wider and walked in. He glanced at his daughter and then at Alexis, they both appeared afraid of him. He bent down on his knees and beckoned his child. She looked back at Alexis and then walked over to him.

"Honey, what are you doing in here? Didn't I tell you that you weren't allowed upstairs?" he scolded her lightly.

"I'm sorry, Daddy, but I heard noises, and I got scared. I didn't see you in the living room so I came up here. But why is she in here? And why is she crying?" Simone pointed to Alexis. She wouldn't tell her daddy that she and the pretty lady had been whispering, and she had a new secret. The lady had asked her for her help and she wanted to help her just like she wanted to help her mommy. She knew her mommy was always afraid of her daddy, but she didn't know why.

Simone blinked and took her daddy's hand. He led her toward the door.

"Come on, let's go back downstairs and leave the pretty lady to herself."

Simone quietly nodded but seemed saddened. She looked back at Alexis, waving to her as her father closed and locked the door. This time he took the key out of the door and put it in his pocket.

🦟 36 🦟

ALEXIS

Alexis held her breath until she heard the lock click. She let her breath out in ragged outbursts. She wouldn't have known what to expect had Sean come into the room a few seconds earlier. He would have seen his daughter give her the toenail clipper. She had noticed it on the dresser when she was scanning the room, looking for an escape. She tried to figure out how she would break the ties with it. She laid there for about a good ten minutes to make sure that Sean wasn't going to come back into the room. She twisted her body just enough to get her hand in the right position. She began clipping the ties until she was able to free her hand. She was just about to try the next one until she heard the key jangling on the other side of the door. She shifted back and pretended to watch TV. Sean walked in carrying a tray of food. She didn't realize she was hungry until she smelled the food.

"If I take those ties off will you behave and eat your food?" he asked her while he had his back to her, placing the tray of food on the dresser.

Oh shit! I can't let him untie me. He would see what I was doing. Thinking quickly, she blurted out, "You know, it would be so much more romantic if you fed me," she said sweetly. Sean looked at her surprised by her comment, but said nothing. He straightened up his face, smiling. Then he brought the tray over to the bed. He set it down lightly and then he sat.

"I'm glad to see you are starting to come around. I hope my daughter didn't bother you too much, but I am glad you've met. I think you are going to be a good stepmother. I always loved how you interacted with the kids on your block. They seemed to really love you. You always looked so happy and carefree when you were around them."

Alexis almost choked on the food she was chewing on. He had been watching her outside of her home? This was too much. She felt the bile rising in her mouth and she choked it back down. Sean assumed it was because of the bread and gave her juice to sip on through a straw. She wondered what else he had been watching her do. At least now, she could explain that feeling in the pit of her stomach. For the next fifteen minutes, he fed her the food he had made, which was her favorite; tuna melt on pretzel bread, strawberries and watermelon. Outside of the juice, he had offered her coffee, which she declined to drink. She made sure she didn't make idle chat with him, but smiled enough times to keep her rouse going. He fed her in silence for a few more minutes. She caught him watching her chew, more than once, while he had this faraway look on his face.

"I have a surprise for you later," he told her. Alexis pretended she hadn't heard him and continued eating.

"I'm full," Alexis said, looking at him full-faced for the first time since he started feeding her. She tried to shift her weight and her arm slipped out. Quickly, she attempted to put it back in, hoping he hadn't seen it. But he had.

"What the hell?" he yelled, getting up quickly and knocking everything to the floor. He grabbed her by the neck and lifted her off the bed.

"So, you're trying to escape, huh? Just how far did you think you would get? You don't even know where we are, Ally, do you? Do you?" he yelled at her.

Alexis hated the pet name he gave her a long time ago.

"Why are you testing my love for you? Haven't I shown you enough? Well, I guess it's time for me to show you what Veronica learned. You need to see what bad behavior gets you," he said, throwing her back on the bed. He unbuttoned his pants and lunged for her. Alexis screamed. Sean grabbed her by the arms and they began to tussle hard. He placed his hand over her mouth so that she couldn't scream again and alarm his daughter. But it was too late. Simone was standing on the side of the bed. Alexis saw her come in, hoping he wouldn't harm her in his fury. His daughter ran to the other side of the bed and yelled at him.

"Daddy! Daddy, stop it! Stop it you're hurting her!" Simone began pounding her small fists on her father's leg, crying. She never had the courage to help her mommy when she heard the screams, but now, she would do something. It took him a few minutes to grasp what was going on. After a few moments, they both stopped, completely out of breath. Sean turned to his daughter and stopped short of smacking the little girl.

"Simone, go downstairs now!" he told her in his stern father voice.

Simone looked at her father and did something they both were surprised at.

"NO, Daddy, NO!" she yelled back at him. She ran around him and straight into Alexis' arms. Alexis felt her anguish as she held the little girl. She rocked her while she buried her head in her chest. The tears and fear in both their eyes stopped him where he stood. Alexis watched him and dared him in silence to come near them. He stepped back instead, got on his knees like he did earlier, and reached for her. She shook her head and held onto Alexis tighter. He tried again to reach out to his daughter and Alexis spoke to her in a quiet tone. The little girl sniffed and turned to look at her father.

"Princess, come here. Daddy's so sorry. I would never hurt you. Come here, please." He motioned to his child a third time, but she didn't move from Alexis' embrace. He stood up and went to the door. He didn't look back at them, but closed the door silently.

"Simone, thank you for helping me. You are such a brave little girl. I have my own personal angel. Where did all that strength come from?" Simone smiled in her innocence. The gesture touched her. It hurt her heart that she had to witness what he was doing to her.

"My Mommy," Simone finally told her.

"Your *mommy*? What do you mean?" Alexis knew his daughter didn't know about her mother's death yet, but she didn't doubt her either.

"My Mommy came to me in my dreams. She said she was gone to heaven, and I had to protect you like she had protected me all this time. She made me promise that I would make sure Daddy didn't hurt you like he had hurt her."

Alexis pulled the child into her arms tighter. They cried together. Sean's selfishness at taking his daughter's mother was unthinkable. Didn't he care if he hurt her?

37

SEAN

Sean put his ear to the door. He couldn't believe what he had heard her say. Veronica came to her in a dream. He never once thought how much this would really affect his daughter. He felt the pain in his soul when he saw how they both looked so afraid of him. Slowly, he walked downstairs and poured himself a shot of Hennessy. It burned. He poured another, swallowing it fast. He put the glass down and wiped the tears from his face. He stared at the tux on the outside of the door. He jumped when the shrill of his phone interrupted the quietness. He grabbed the phone up and spoke. It was the pastor telling him he would be there within the hour. He started to tell him never mind, but didn't. He still wanted Alexis as his wife. All this was for her, and he had come too far not to finish it to the end. Walking into his daughter's room, he grabbed her dress and accessories. Sean would not reattempt to have Simone come with him. He felt it was best to leave them the way they were, he wouldn't force her to leave Alexis. Taking the stairs two at a time, he opened the door and found them both where he had left them, almost thirty minutes ago. He set her clothes on the chair and sat on the bed. All three sat in silence. He spoke calmly.

"Why do you insist on betraying me? This isn't what I wanted...the fear you two have against me. No, it's not. But ... but ... I can't live without either of you. Please don't try and cross me again." Scooting back on the bed, he saw both of them flinch. He went back to his original spot. His heart tightened.

"The pastor will be here soon. Can you both get dressed? I will be back up here to get you." He walked out of the room, locking the door behind him.

38

ZAVIER

Zavier waited for his superior to reply. Ain't no way he was referring to him as father. Sims looked uncomfortable, "I just wanted to be here for you. I wanted to be able to talk, you never would give me the chance to explain anything to you."

"Explain? Is that what you were going to do? I mean I've always thought my father was dead. Looking at you now doesn't change that thought much."

"Zavier..."

"What?! What can you possibly say!" he yelled, interrupting him. The small action drained the little energy he had from his rest.

"I don't know. I didn't want it to be this way. When I found out I was sick, the first thing I wanted to do was tell you and Terrance. I didn't want to carry that burden to my grave."

"Do you think it would make a difference now?"

"According to you it doesn't. But to me, at least you know. Now I just have to tell Terrance."

"Tell me what?" Terrance said walking in the door, and both men looked at him. Zavier spoke first in the deafening silence. "Tell him!"

"Tell me what? What is going on?" Terrance asked waiting for either of them to respond. The Commander looked at Zavier who put his head down. "I... I am your father, and you and Zavier are brothers."

"What? What the hell did you just say?" Terrance's face showed clear shock and anger.

"I'm sorry. I didn't want this to happen this way. I didn't want... you..." Commander Sims struggled to finish as he clutched his chest and fell to his knees. Terrance opened the door calling for a nurse as Zavier tried to sit up but wasn't able to. "Commander, Commander!" both men called out to him as a nurse and a doctor rushed in and began performing CPR on him. Within seconds he was placed on a gurney and rushed out of the room. Terrance hurried behind them and left Zavier in the room alone. He didn't completely understand what just happened. He wished he could get up and go see, but he had to sit there and wait. Was this his fault too?

❦ 39 ❦

SEAN

S ean was getting dressed, but he was clearly distracted as Alexis'
words rang out in his head. He replayed the conversation in his
head when he had asked her why she couldn't love him.

"*Sean, how could you even expect me to fall for you? You have done nothing
but hurt me. What woman falls in love with the one person who has taken
almost everything from her that matters? You killed my father and tried to kill
my fiancé. Look, look at your daughter. She is so afraid of you. You stole from her
too and she can't replace that with me. Did you even think about this? You have
scarred her for life, and no amount of healing will ever make it go away. No
band-aid will ever be able to cover her wounds. No. No. I could never love you.
You're selfish! You've made this all about what you wanted. It wasn't about me;
it wasn't about your wife, or your daughter. This was all about Sean. You make
me sick, literally. You make my stomach turn,*" she had told him, never
backing down as she looked him straight in his eyes. Sean started to
balk at her words but he couldn't, it was the first time they had actually
affected him. Looking at his reflection he tried to see the person she
spoke of. The man she had said was so selfish she got sick. Was *he* a
monster? Out of nowhere, he started laughing. She was good, very
good, he thought. For a moment, he let her get into his mind. He
almost let her get him off balance. Of course, he wasn't any of those

130

things she claimed him to be. He made a mental note to tell her how great her academy performance was. He fixed his tux and double-checked himself in the mirror. He was handsome, smart, and most of all, he was a loving man. His daughter always told him that. She was his little angel, and she would be okay with Alexis as her new mom. The things that happened today would blow over, and Simone and Alexis would both be putty in his hands after the wedding. Simone never should have had to witness what happened upstairs. Another sign that he was slipping. He was going to make his daughter love him again. Causing her to fear him was never his intention. He would fix it, fix it all. This was just the beginning, he thought as he ran his hands over his tuxedo. Glancing at himself in the mirror again, he saw the man he knew he was, not the one that Alexis claimed he was.

Making his own mind up, he continued to run with those thoughts. Whistling, he went upstairs to get the girls. It was almost that time. He had to admit, he was so glad that she bonded with Simone. It made all this a whole lot easier, knowing they would get along well. He had just done all that worrying for nothing.

❧ 40 ❧

ALEXIS

Alexis watched his back with her mouth agape. Then she pinched herself. She had to be dreaming, she slowly convinced herself. She couldn't believe that after everything she had spewed at him that he still wanted to go through with this. Nothing she ever did in her life could have prepared her for this man and his drive to make her his wife.

Simone glanced at her and the dress her father brought in. Alexis sighed heavily, realizing she had to oblige until she figured out a way to get them out of this house safely. She picked up Simone and held her, reassuring her that everything would be okay. Alexis' mind began to become active as a plan formed in her head. Lifting Simone's chin she spoke to her. "Okay, baby, I think I know what we can do. You think you are up to helping me?"

"Yes, I can do whatever you want me to," Simone told her

"Okay, so, this is what we are going to do. I am going to distract your daddy when we get downstairs together. I just want you to look for my signal okay?"

She explained to her what they needed to do. Simone nodded.

Alexis finished putting the final hair accessories in Simone's hair.

She was going to do what she needed to do, to get them through this and keep them both calm and cool. The two talked the whole time. She learned that Simone was seven years old and loved playing dress up. Alexis told her that's what they were doing; that all three of them were pretending, and she reminded her that all she had to do was follow her lead. Her new little friend agreed again. It was all settled. Looking over to the door, she looked at the dress before getting up.

Taking the dress off the hanger, she wanted to flush it down the toilet. Slowly, so she wouldn't freak out, she put the dress over her head and got ready for whatever it was that was supposed to take place. How did he manage to get a marriage license from the court without her, let alone someone to agree to perform the ceremony? She had just finished glossing their lips when they heard the door. Alexis and Simone decided they were not giving Sean their power and wouldn't be afraid or show him they were afraid, or even flinch anymore when he came around. Hugging Simone quickly, they stood, waiting on him to enter. They both heard the door click and then slowly open. Sean stood in the doorway dressed up as fancy as they were. Alexis tried not to get sick and swallowed the bile forming in her throat. Simone watched her daddy and then looked at Alexis, who squeezed her hand a little.

Sean stepped into the room and did a double take. Looking at them both, his eyes watered. That caught Alexis off guard, but she made no verbal comment. Sean walked farther into the room, holding his hand out to his daughter. She hesitated; making sure it was still okay with Alexis who nodded slightly. Letting go of Alexis' hand, Simone took his hand slowly and he twirled her around. She giggled, remembering how much she loved when her daddy twirled her. It must have been something they did often Alexis thought watching them. Once he finished, Sean's eyes took in her whole dress and makeup. He backed up and just stared at her. Alexis started to feel very uncomfortable under his scrutiny. Clearing her throat, she thwarted his attention. He was wearing a grey tuxedo; the blue rose that was stuck in his lapel matched the blue roses that were on both her and Simone's dress. He was very detailed. He went to the closet and pulled a clear bag out. Tearing the plastic off, the veil he had for her was covered with imprinted butterflies and blue roses. He handed the veil to Simone and picked her up. His daughter placed it gently on Alexis' hair. He put her down and put the veil in place.

"You look very beautiful. I knew you would. You almost take my breath away," he said gently.

Alexis wondered how he could go from hot and cold in a matter of seconds. She shivered in spite of herself. He asked Simone to walk ahead of them as he came over and swept Alexis in his arms. In doing so, a loud thud followed. Looking down, she saw the black handle of his gun. Swallowing hard, she prayed silently.

Sean skillfully squatted and retrieved his gun, never missing a step.

"It's time we made this official, so we can get out of town."

Her whole body shook under his touch as he carried her down the stairs. She silently prayed and cried out for Zavier. She couldn't believe this man really expected them to exchange vows. He sat her on the couch and Simone followed suit without instruction. He quickly tucked the gun in his back waist before Simone noticed. She was playing with one of her dolls he had left on the couch for her.

The doorbell chimed, and three pairs of eyes went to the door. Sean didn't move immediately as he checked his watch.

"Let me go get that. Behave ladies. I have eyes everywhere," he warned.

Alexis took the opportunity to quickly go over what they had talked about. "Simone, remember what we talked about," she whispered. "Watch for the signals, okay? You have to be quick."

Simone nodded and reached up and kissed her cheek.

"Don't be scared. We will get through this. We have our own watchers," she told her, pointing upward. Speechless, she said nothing. The little girl's comment made her tear up. There were no words she could say behind that. Hearing the men, she quickly came up with a plan B of her own, just in case. Simone leaned into her and waited.

"Whatever happens today or in the future, I want you to know you have a friend in me always, and you can talk to me anytime, okay?" she whispered into her ear. Simone nodded and hugged her.

"You know, I still don't know your name," Simone said quietly.

Alexis frowned, but realized the child was right. She could have sworn Sean had used her name in front of her, but just dismissed the thought as she spoke softly to her.

"It's Alexis."

"Okay, Ms. Alexis."

Hearing the footsteps come closer to them on the wooden floor, they both watched as Sean and his guest came back into the room. Alexis gasped inconspicuously. She regarded the man in the face and knew instantly they were saved. She recognized him as one of Zavier and Terrance's Mason brothers. At least that is what he had been introduced to her as. She had been found, she thought, relieved. The man gave a blank look as they were introduced. He shook her hand as if they were meeting for the first time. Knowing he was playing a part, she followed suit and shook his hand lightly. Afterwards, Sean spoke to the pastor in a hushed tone for several minutes and then proceeded to have her and Simone stand for the ceremony. As the man in disguise went on to say that he needed them to sign the certificate before they could proceed, she could see Sean's jaw twitch. He must have forgotten about that as he looked at his watch and then nodded at the man. He stood there momentarily, as if contemplating the pastor's request.

"Sean, a few more minutes isn't going to make a difference," she told him, playing along because she knew this would be over before they said *I do*. At least she hoped it would.

He nodded his understanding to his soon-to-be wife. He looked at the pastor and nodded his head for the man to get the paperwork.

The pastor reached into the briefcase he was carrying and instead of paperwork, he pulled out a gun.

"Sean, the house is surrounded. Put your hands up now!" the man yelled. He stepped closer and then paused as he kept guarding Sean's reaction. Alexis stood frozen.

"What the hell is this?!" Sean exclaimed, looking at the pastor in a wild-eyed manner.

"Don't make this harder than it has to be. Think about your little girl over there," he said as he slowly walked again in a small circle, making sure to keep them all in sight.

Sean tightened his jaws. Alexis knew he wasn't going to make this easy. She eyed Simone, giving her one of the signals. Simone screamed as she was told to do, creating the diversion. The room's mood quickly changed, and things looked like they were going in slow motion.

✺ 41 ✺

ZAVIER

Zavier looked over at the digital clock on the wall. It had been over an hour since his superior had collapsed and was taken out of his hospital room. He watched the door and tapped his hand nervously on the arm rail. He couldn't get that one question out of his mind; the one question he had asked himself when he was taken from his room. Was this his fault? Was his anger toward him the reason he had collapsed? Finally, he decided to push his call button to find out something. He didn't know anything about the commander or Alexis and he'd had enough of the quietness in the room. Moving over in his bed he searched for the call button; finding it he was just about to push it when his door opened. He quickly looked up as Terrance entered, he walked straight into the room and over to his bed. When he didn't say anything he spoke, "What happened? Is the commander okay?" Terrance shook his head, but still said nothing. "Come on man, tell me something!" Zavier said getting frustrated with him not telling him anything. Was his best friend mad at him, or should he be calling him brother? Terrance finally spoke, but he could barely make out what he was saying.

"He's...he's...in ICU. But it doesn't look good."

"What? Terrance, I can barely hear you," he told him, hoping he would repeat himself.

Looking at him like they didn't know one another, he repeated himself. "He is in ICU and it doesn't look good, but what the hell was going on when I walked in?"

"That's not important. Get me outta here. Can we talk to the doctors or something? I just want to go see about him and then go home and find Alexis," Zavier told him. He wanted to avert talking about this anymore, it made him feel somewhat better to know he wasn't dead. He would deal with the other part later. He just didn't realize how soon later would be. Terrance turned around and walked out without a word.

Zavier was waiting on Terrance to come back into the room. The nurse had just given him his discharge instructions. The patient care assistant wheeled the chair in and he slowly stepped off the bed and into the waiting seat. He let out a hard breath as he was wheeled out into the hallway. When they reached the elevator they were met by Terrance. "Sorry, I went to go check on the commander, he's awake and asked if we could both come in for a second." Zavier looked up at Terrance, he didn't know what to say, so he just nodded his head yes. He had just wanted to make sure he was okay, before he left. Seeing him wasn't in his immediate plans. Terrance stood in place of the assistant as he stepped out of the way and wheeled Zavier in the direction he had just left. When they entered in Commander Sims' room they were greeted with beeps, and lights going on and off signaling his care. Commander Sims was sitting up, but his eyes were not opened.

"Commander, we are here," Terrance said softly in his direction as he wheeled Zavier closer to the bed. Commander Sims opened his eyes and gave a slight smile. Neither man smiled in return. He began talking softly, "Thank you, thank for coming. I just wanted to finish what I started earlier, before it is too late. First, I want to say I'm sorry. Sorry that things turned out the way they did and that you both are finding out the way you are. I never meant to hurt anyone, and that includes your mothers as well as you both," he started. Terrance's face twisted up. He looked from the commander to Zavier, then back to the commander. "Our mothers? What do they have to do with this?" Terrance interrupted.

"That's...that's what I have been trying to tell you. I had a relationship with both of your mothers. I loved them both. Leslie didn't know, but when she found out, it tore them apart. It... was... all my fault. And I take full blame for that." Commander Sims continued slowly, he took a sudden deep breath and a machine began to beep louder. A nurse hurried into the room within seconds, followed by another nurse who began speaking to them in a rushed voice.

"Gentlemen, please step back for a moment," she told them as they went about the room checking the monitors and then Commander Sims. Terrance did what she said as he pulled the chair out of the way and to the side some. Terrance didn't understand his comment, but kept his composure as much as he could. They both heard the commander say something softly, but then louder as the nurse were checking him out.

"No, no. I have to finish talking to them," he told the one nurse as he tried to swat her hand away from him.

"Sir, please let me do my job. I'm trying to prolong your life."

"I don't care about that, please let me finish talking to them, give, give me ten seconds, then do what you must." The nurse looked from his pleading eyes to Zavier and Terrance, and slowly stepped to the side but she didn't leave the room. Terrance again wheeled Zavier and himself closer to his bed. Commander Sims wasted no time in finishing, "You two are my sons."

"What! What did you just say," Terrance said with shock in his voice.

Zavier ran his hand over his face.

"You are my sons. Please, please don't let it tear you apart like it did your mothers. I care for and love you both even if you didn't know the truth," Commander Sims said and soon after the machine beeped loudly as his eyes slowly closed. The nurse once again moved in quickly as this time she was joined by the other nurse and doctor who had rushed into the room within moments of the machine beeping. They began to work on the commander trying to resuscitate him. They tried for almost ten minutes before the doctor finally called for them to stop, and pronounced him dead. Zavier wiped the tear from his face with his good hand. He heard a noise from Terrance but couldn't make out what it was. This wasn't what he needed. It was just too much. Without another word, Terrance opened the hospital room door and quickly wheeled him out of the room and to the elevator. He held on to the sides in fear of the way he was being pushed so that he wouldn't end up on the floor, but he didn't say a word. When they got to the main entrance, Terrance wheeled him over to his truck and helped him into the passenger seat. The ride to his house was quiet. They both heard Terrance's phone going off repeatedly. He didn't make a move to answer it. The other UNIT members must have been notified, but how?

Once they made it to his home, Terrance once again helped him out the truck and into his house. He helped him onto the couch. Pacing the room for a few seconds, he looked over at Zavier, and stopped. "You knew, didn't you?" He wasn't mad with the question, at least he didn't sound mad. Zavier answered, "Yeah, that's what was in that envelope you gave me the other day."

"I need some air. I'm sorry I know you need me, but I need to digest all of this. I will get a status on Alexis from Dobbs, he is who we sent in and he should be back in a little while. Will you be okay?"

Zavier nodded. What could he say? He didn't want him to leave him alone, but it wasn't like he didn't understand. He still hadn't digested it either. He didn't want to. He was focusing on his fiancée. Picking up his phone, he texted the detective and just waited.

He had been home for nearly four hours and was antsy. They were coming up on twenty-four hours since Sean had kidnapped Alexis. He didn't know how much longer he was going to be able to keep his cool. He hadn't slept since he'd been home. His phone had gone off repeatedly in regard to Commander Sims, but Terrance still had not been back and wasn't responding to his calls. It had been nearly an hour and Zavier didn't know what he could do; he just felt helpless. Adjusting himself he heard a couple knocks, he got up slowly and headed to the door, wincing a little from the pain in his side and arm. He was wired all of a sudden for some reason. He opened the door to Harris, one of the other UNIT members. He had come to check in on him.

"What's up, man? Anything?" he asked Harris, hoping he didn't look as frantic as he was sounding. Harris walked into his apartment more and he followed slowly but steadily behind him, until they reached where he was originally in his living room. He finally spoke.

"Dobbs and Terrance found a few things in Sean's house. It was all given to the detective. He's checking into it and will get back with us. But Dobbs is doing more than anyone, and we haven't been able to reach him. But it should be okay, I know you don't want to hear this but I need you to calm down and sit, please. You know you should be resting. If you have a relapse, what good will you be to your girl then?" his friend scolded, trying to get Zavier to be still for more than a few minutes.

"I can't. Not until she is in my arms," he said, looking him dead in the face.

"Wow, so she is really the one?" Harris questioned him

"Yes, she is," he said, surprised that he would even ask, after all he was doing. His friend didn't know Alexis like Terrance did, although he didn't spend much time with her either. He knew Terrance wouldn't question the obvious. Smiling as he envisioned Alexis' smile that he was missing so much.

Harris cleared his throat, bringing Zavier back to the present.

"I have some other information for you. Commander Sims had me in his office yesterday, he had me taking care of something confidential for him, but he told me it was for you. When we got the news about the commander I remembered I had the papers, I was going to give them to him tomorrow morning." Handing them to him he watched to see if he was going to open them. He was curious why they were so secret, and why Commander Sims had been so adamant about them.

Zavier hesitated when he heard the name, recalling the vision of watching him die right in front of him. He still needed to address that issue, no matter how much he wanted to keep it in the back of his mind. The UNIT wasn't going to let him do it and through it all Commander Sims deserved his respect, even if he could never address him as father.

Zavier's hand started shaking as he opened the sealed letter and read over the document. His friend watched his face as he finished reading. Neither man said anything as his eyes darted over the letter and its content.

Zavier's cell phone buzzed on the table. He didn't immediately reach for it. He had waited years for the chance to be free and clear of his past. This paper had done that. He folded it, just as both he and his friend's phone rang at the same time. Zavier greeted Detective Spencer, but had a hard time hearing him. "Detective, I can't hear you!" There was a lot of background noise, voices he couldn't understand followed by some gunshots. Then the line went dead. All the color drained out of his face, as he let the phone slide out of his hand. He didn't care that it landed on the phone. He could have sworn for a second he had heard Alexis scream.

Terrance walked into his house just as the other man ended his call. They both looked over at him. Terrance looked disheveled. Zavier knew why, but the other guy assumed it was because of Commander Sims' passing. "Hey, man, are you okay?" he asked Zavier but was still watching Terrance. "It was Detective Spencer. I heard..." Zavier started and both men flew into action.

Terrance's demeanor changed quickly and he turned back into his best friend. "What happened? What did you hear?" Terrance quizzed

"I... I couldn't tell."

"Think! Use your training skills," Terrance spoke sternly to Zavier and that got him out of his trance. He closed his eyes, recalling what he'd heard. "There was a lot of wind ...clanking sounds, voices. Yes, voices. I think one of them was Alexis. She was screaming. Then I heard a bunch of gunshots before the line went dead."

"Good, you did good. Now, take this, and I will be back shortly," Terrance told him as he handed him a cup of juice. He failed to mention he had crushed his pain pill in with it. He needed him to relax so that they could finish this out. Terrance and their other partner stepped quickly out of his house. Terrance looked back as he closed the door.

It didn't take long for Zavier's eyes to feel heavy. He heard his townhome door close. The tears fell from his eyes as the pain pill started to kick in.

✸ 42 ✸

TERRANCE

Terrance sped away from Zavier's place, and headed straight to the one place he had always felt peace. Even if he had never been there during the night. He knew he needed to go. Making a left turn Terrance went through the front entrance of Hillside Cemetery. Driving to where he had always gone, when he came to see his mother's grave. Parking, he slowly got out of his truck and walked over to her tombstone. Looking at her name Leslie D. Cross. Pulling some of the grass away he kneeled. Touching her tombstone, the tears flowed from his eyes. "So, is this what you didn't want me to know, what I begged for you to tell me before you went to heaven? Did you think I would be mad? That I wouldn't understand?" he whispered to her tombstone, pausing like he was expecting her to answer. "Mama, I love you I promise I am not mad at you, but I could have handled it, I know I could have. I have looked up to Commander Sims most of my life, I... I know it wasn't supposed to come out like this. I will get through this, and I hope you and auntie will too since you are all together. Forgive her, and yeah even forgive him mama." He spoke to his mother as he kissed his fingers and then touched her tombstone once more. Wiping his face, he gets up, and heads back to his car. He didn't know how long he had been sitting there staring out in space just thinking, until the security car rode up on him. The guard clicked his lights on and off to get his attention. Terrance blinked his eyes and rolled his window down showing his badge he pulled off his side. Starting his car, the guard acknowledged him as he drove on the opposite side of him. Looking at his clock on the dashboard, he had been sitting there for almost three hours. His pain was deep, but it was more because he felt cheated. He saw the anger in Zavier, but he felt different. He was surprised but he wasn't against the confession. At least he knew now that he has some real family. He and Zavier had acted like brothers for years, now they really were. He smiled at that thought, as Commander Sims came back into his mind. Coughing he put his truck in gear and headed back to Zavier's, they should talk he thought, now that he had fully digested everything.

❧ 43 ❧

SEAN

Sean looked down at his daughter as she dashed around him and straight out the door, the pastor had just come into. He strained his neck some to see if he could see where she had gone. Alexis had more than likely told her to hide. Furious, Sean still attempted to call out his daughter's name.

"Simone! Simone, get your butt back in here," he yelled, but she didn't come back. How did Alexis manage to get his daughter to turn her back on him? Then he remembered the look of fear she gave him earlier and knew he was the cause of her betrayal. Again, he tried to see if he could spot her outside through the window. His daughter was nowhere in his immediate eyesight. Silently cursing under his breath. He looked over to Alexis, giving her a cold look of hate; all he had done for her and she still betrayed him, he then quickly gave a side eyes look at the so-called pastor. He stood up taller making his presence seem bigger than it was as he directed his anger at the man, who had pretended to be someone he wasn't.

"Who the hell are you?" he asked, furious now for different reasons. The man didn't reply, only cocked his gun. Quickly, Sean grabbed Alexis and went to reach for his own gun. He was completely distracted when he realized his hand was empty and his gun wasn't there. Looking around wildly, he searched for it, while he tried to keep his eyes on them both.

"Sean, let her go, and let's end this peacefully," the pastor told him.

"Fuck you, whoever you are!" he spat at him. He began backing up, finally seeing where he had put his gun. Walking toward it, and dragging Alexis, he grabbed it and placed it up to Alexis' head. She yanked and tried to get away. Sean tightened his grip around her neck. She began to slightly gag.

"I will kill her. Put your gun down now!" Sean shouted.

The pastor did not relent and Sean cocked his gun and pressed it harder into her skull. Alexis whimpered in fear.

"Put your gun down now!" he repeated.

The pastor slowly proceeded to put his gun down. Sean started moving toward the bedroom, again practically dragging Alexis with him. He kissed her face. "This was all for you. I am not selfish like you said. This is all for you!" he gestured wildly to make his point. The pastor took baby steps to follow them. Sean stopped in his tracks once Simone appeared behind the pastor. She picked up the pastor's gun. She pointed it in the direction of Sean and Alexis.

"Daddy, this is for my Mommy." Simone closed her eyes and pulled the trigger as hard as she could, the impact from the gun knocked the little girl back in the hall... then everything suddenly went in slow motion as the room erupted in sounds of gunfire and screams.

✦ 44 ✦

ALEXIS

Alexis' ears were ringing. She opened her eyes. The room smelled like blood, flesh, and gunfire. She pushed at Sean's dead body weight as she attempted to get up. Suddenly, sharp pain hit the top of her shoulder. The wedding dress felt heavy. It was saturated with blood. Sean's eyes were open, but his brain matter was smeared all on the floor. Positioning her good arm, she used it to crawl away from his body as much as she could. Where was Simone? Forgetting her pain, she got on all fours, calling out to her. "Simone, sweetie, where are you? Honey, you can come out! Simone, please come out!" She continued calling her name. Her leg hit a body. She was expecting it to be the pastor, but when she reached down and turned his face; she saw that it was Detective Spencer. Moaning, he tried to open his eyes. She carefully lifted his head and placed it onto her lap. She grabbed the only towel that was in her reach pressing down on his stomach.

"We got him. I promised you we would get him, Alexis," he said barely audible. He coughed slightly and blood spilled out his mouth as he closed his eyes.

"Detective! Detective Spencer, please hold on," she whispered as her tears fell on his face. Suddenly the door burst open and uniformed officers flooded the room racing around in all different directions, finally shining a light in her face. The officer lowered the light, as he and the other officers took in the scene. She heard the sirens seconds later. Soon an EMT was standing over here, trying to urge her to get up. She didn't want to leave Detective Spencer. "Ma'am, I can't work on him if you won't help me. Please come on. It will be okay," The EMT told her as he escorted her to one of the waiting ambulances. Looking over her shoulder, she said a quick prayer for him. The scene outside was just as busy, and she still didn't see Simone. The tech had just given her a shot when she heard Simone calling her name.

"Ms. Alexis, I did it. I killed Daddy so he wouldn't kill you. I shot my Daddy," she cried to her as she laid her head on her stomach. Alexis tried to comfort her as much as she could.

45

ZAVIER

Zavier walked back and forth as much as he could through his pain, wiping the sweat off his face. When he woke up he was alone and truly upset. Terrance had him drink that juice to calm down. He guessed it worked but what he wanted to do was be active and find Alexis. He knew Dobbs was a good man for the job, and he didn't fault his skills, but it was just his character. Alexis was his fiancée, so he was the one who was supposed to be keeping her safe, not everyone else. He had just finally gone and sat down when he heard a key in his door. He stood there staring, waiting on Terrance to come thru the door so that he could question him. And as soon as he did, he didn't hesitate.

"Terrance, what's going on? Did you all find her? Is she okay?" he asked one question after another.

Terrance put his hand up to halt him. "Whoa, man, slow down. Are you going to give me a chance to even answer you?"

"Okay, I am listening?"

"First, yes she was found. Second, Detective Spencer and Dobbs both were shot. They are all at the hospital. I came to pick you up."

"Okay, let's go you can tell me how they are, on the way," he told him as he literally pushed him towards the door. Terrance grabbed a few things off the counter and they headed out. He didn't tell him the ride was almost four hours away. Once Terrance helped him in the car, they drove in silence for a few blocks, and then Terrance started talking, but it wasn't about what he wanted to hear. "You do know that we have to talk about Commander Sims at some point. We need to talk about the things he told us and how we go forward."

"Go forward? Are things going to change between you and me? I mean we have always acted like brothers, now it's just official."

"You know what I mean."

"No, I don't. In my eyes nothing changes. I am sorry we lost the commander, I really am. But I can't sit here and pretend that I am happy and excited to know who my father is, like I told him. Right now, my feelings won't change on that. I will go and pay my respects, but that's it man. And frankly it's also the end of this discussion," he said folding his arms over his chest like a young child.

Terrance just looked at him and didn't say anything for the next thirty minutes.

46

TERRANCE

Terrance wanted to be mad at Zavier's behavior about all this. He wanted him to feel the same way he did about it. Relieved at least to know, and not just continue to wonder who his father was, like he did growing up. A part of him agreed with his demeanor, but they were different in all the rest. He sighed, and just decided he would let it just play out as it would. He wouldn't say anything else about it. Speaking, he was going to update him about Spencer and Dobbs as he knew. "Here's what I know about Dobbs and Spencer; they both were injured badly. Spencer is in surgery and Dobbs suffered two bullet wounds; one to the thigh and the other to his shoulder. Sean is dead. And Alexis was grazed by a bullet, but she will be okay, and luckily Simone, Sean's daughter, didn't get hurt at all."

"Wow! Who...who shot Sean?"

"I never got a clear answer to that, so maybe we will both find out together."

Nodding, Zavier turned his attention back to the front as Terrance gave his full attention back to the road. The GPS monitor said they had forty-five minutes until they made it to the hospital. The rest of the ride they remained silent. Terrance was all in his thoughts, he did want to talk more about their father, but he decided it may not be a wise decision to try and talk about it more, since Zavier was so against it.

47

ZAVIER

Zavier had closed his eyes, and must have drifted off a bit. He felt Terrance tapping his arm letting him know they had made it to the hospital. Terrance left him off at the Emergency Room entrance and then went to park. Zavier waited. After a couple minutes he saw Terrance jogging up to meet him. They walked in looking around for anyone familiar. The only person they saw was Dobb's wife. She was crying in a corner, both men headed in her direction. "Nicole, where is everyone? How is Dobbs?" Zavier asked her as he gave her a hug and waited for her response.

"I don't know, they won't give me any information. All I know is he is in surgery but I don't know much of anything else." She told him. Zavier looked over to Terrance and then they both reassured her they would find out something and come back and update her. Heading to the elevators they were greeted by three police officers. They both showed their ID, one of the officers nodded in acceptance, and they proceeded to where they could find out something. Zavier just wanted to see Alexis. When they reached the floor, it was busy with additional officers, nurses and doctors. Terrance went in one direction, and he went slowly but steady in the other direction. He stopped one nurse and gave her Alexis' name. He was pointed to her room which was a few feet from him. Pushing her door opened, the first thing he saw was a little girl around six or seven years old lying in the bed with Alexis. Next, he fixed his eyes on her and his eyes immediately filled. He couldn't understand the emotions that just took over him seeing Alexis laying there. Walking further into the room he was almost to the bed when the little girl woke up, she didn't say anything but she just looked frightened. "Hey there, sweetie. How are you? I'm Zavier, Alexis' soon to be husband. I won't hurt you. I just want to check on Alexis, is that okay with you?" Simone looked back at the sleeping Alexis and then back at him and just laid there looking at him. She finally nodded and went back to her original sleeping position and closed her eyes. Zavier touched her hair, and then placed his hand on Alexis, she moved but didn't open her eyes. And that's when he saw it, the huge bandage on her shoulder; anger immediately filled him. Alexis had gotten hurt. He couldn't tell to what extent, but the mere fact that she was hurt period, he didn't like it at all. "Alexis... Alexis honey, wake up," he whispered near her ear. Again Alexis moved, he could see her eyes flutter and her looking around. Her eyes immediately focused on Simone. Within seconds she looked up and saw Zavier.

"Zav, oh my God! Is that you?"

"Yes, baby, it's me."

"How...how did you know I was here?"

"I have my ways," he told her chuckling lightly.

"Wait! Aren't you hurt? What happened to you?"

"I will be okay. I got hit but my vest saved my life?"

"*Vest?* You were wearing your vest that night? I am so glad to hear that," she told him. Alexis tried to shift her weight without disturbing the sleeping Simone. Zavier watched her caring for the child with her, and knew they had grown attached to each other in the short time they were together. He didn't say anything until he saw her wince with pain. Then he was reminded quickly that she had been hurt. "How are you feeling? I see you got injured."

"I am okay for the most part, but I... I want to know."

"Know what?"

"Is he really dead?" she whispered so Simone wouldn't hear her.

"Yes. Yes, he is gone and he can't hurt anyone else."

Covering her mouth, she let out a sigh, leaning her head onto the child, she hugged her softly. Looking back at him she looked puzzled.

"What's wrong, Alexis?"

"Where is Detective Spencer? And what about the pastor? Are they...are they all right? She asked slowly.

"I don't know just yet. Terrance went to check and I came in here to see you first."

"Oh, okay," she told him through a quivering voice, the tears had started falling now.

Reaching over, Zavier wiped her tears away with his thumb, he leaned over them both and kissed his fiancée. The kiss was just as sweet as it always was, but it was filled with both of their present emotions.

"I love you," he told her when the kiss ended.

"I love you too. Thank you for being here with me and for helping me. I couldn't have gotten through this without you. It's no telling where I would be at this time," she told him touching his face.

Neither of them had noticed that Simone was fully awake and watching them. They all turned when the door opened and an older woman walked in, sad, but happy to see Simone.

"Nana!!" she screamed when the woman came closer. Zavier helped her down and she ran the short distance to her, they both cried as they hugged. Zavier watched the exchange and knew Alexis was in even more tears. When they stopped hugging, the woman extended her hand to Zavier and then to Alexis. Introducing herself as Brenda, Simone's grandmother and the mother of the now deceased wife of Sean. "I just want to say thank you, thank you for keeping Simone safe, I don't know what I would do if I lost her too."

"You are very welcome. Simone has a new lifetime friend in me, and so do you. Please keep in touch with us."

"I truly will," she told her. Zavier pulled a business card out of his wallet and wrote down Alexis' number and handed over the card afterwards. Simone came back over to where Alexis was in the bed. She reached up and hugged Alexis as hard as she could. Zavier smiled, knowing that in spite of everything that happened, these two would have each other.

⚬⚬⚬

IT HAD BEEN ALMOST THIRTY MINUTES SINCE SIMONE AND HER grandmother had left. Zavier had been sitting next to Alexis. Neither one of them had spoken much. He held her hand the whole time. He was just happy to be next to her, and for some reason the vision of Commander Sims entered his mind. His words of confession replayed in his mind.

As if she sensed his thoughts, Alexis squeezed his hand some, "Zav, what's wrong?"

"How did you know?"

"I just do. I know you better than you know yourself sometimes," she told him, and those words cut through his core. He had always thought he was doing a good job on masking his past, but maybe he wasn't doing as good as he assumed.

"I have something to tell you. I found out who my father was."

"Your father? When did this happen?"

"This week."

"Zavier, who is it?"

"You will never believe this. It's um, Commander Sims, but that's only part of it."

"You mean there's more? Okay, I am listening."

"Terrance is my brother, and I mean my half-brother. Commander Sims is both of our father."

"Wow! How are you handling this? Will you be spending time with him? What about Terrance? How is he handling this?"

"Well, much better than me. But there is one other small but big piece. He died last night at the hospital when he was coming to check in on me. That's how Terrance found out. He told us both everything right before he suffered a heart attack."

"Zavier, I am so sorry. This is all too much. Me, Sean, and now you finding out who your father was and losing him all in the same week,"

"Yeah, but I will be okay as long as I have you."

"Zavier, of course, you have me, but you have to face this. Please don't push it to the side. We have been through a lot these last few weeks. Don't hold your feelings in please."

"Alexis, I'm okay."

"Are you? I am sure you don't want to talk about this, so I appreciate you even sharing this with me."

"Alexis, I will be okay eventually. I promise, the shock is still wearing off. And now he is gone, I can't ask him anything, but I guess working with him for over ten years helps some; I know what kind of man he was. The best part is having Terrance as an official brother, we will get through everything else."

"Okay, Zavier. You know I am here for you and for Terrance. I hope you plan on attending the service?"

"I wasn't, but if you are up to going, I will."

"Of course, I will," she told him just as there was a knock on the hospital room door.

Terrance walked in and came over to the couple. "Alexis, I'm glad you are okay."

"Thank you, Terrance, and thank you for helping Zav after he was shot. I can't tell you how much it means to me."

"No doubt, that's my *brother*," he said proudly.

Zavier smiled. He knew Terrance meant every part of what he had just said. Zavier couldn't exactly speak at the moment, looking at Alexis and then Terrance, he had his family right in this room with him, and he wouldn't change that for anything.

EPILOGUE

TWO MONTHS LATER...

Alexis parked her car in front of her studio. The whole ride in she had tried to keep her thoughts away from the things that had literally changed her life. Alexis was luckier than most women in her position, including Sean's wife. She and Zavier had attended her funeral. Her death had hurt her like she had known the woman. No matter what she knew, and who she had the misfortune of marrying, she didn't deserve to die, and in her mind, she would feel like she was at some fault, even if she really wasn't.

Sean was a very unbalanced man. She should have made sure he was locked up for good after he killed her father; but that was out of her control as well. Quickly wiping the tear that had just rolled down her face, she closed her eyes briefly getting herself together. Taking a deep breath, she grabbed her purse and opened the door to get out of the car, locking the door behind her. Alexis walked slowly to the front entrance, standing there for a few moments before she unlocked the studio door. She was glad she had taken some time before returning, this was her first day back in the studio since the ordeal with Sean. She pushed the door open, turning the lights on. She looked all around and for the first time in a long time, she felt calm. She headed in the direction of her dance room. Glad to be back doing what she loved doing. She wanted to resume some type of normalcy as much as she could.

Turning on the light, she was greeted by a room full of people, yelling, "Surprise!" Clapping her hands over her mouth, she laughed. It was another first for her; she had not laughed in a long time.

There was a huge *WELCOME BACK* sign and all of her old coworkers, her students and her small family were in attendance. The tears flowed down her face. Her husband handed the bouquet of flowers to Simone, and she ran to Alexis, passing her the arrangement of lilies and orchids and giving her a big hug. Simone's grandmother was in the crowd crying as well. Alexis and Simone had become extremely close. She never knew a braver child, and despite all that she had been through, she was managing to adjust very well, without her parents. It was rough for a little while as Simone was convinced that she had shot and killed her father. Alexis had thought the same thing until Zavier finally told her what really happened after she got home and things settled down some. When Simone picked up the pastor's gun, she thought she had fired the fatal shot. She had heard the blast and saw her father fall, just as a bullet tore through Alexis' shoulder, but in actuality, Detective Spencer was standing behind her and had shot Sean twice.

When Sean hit the floor, he was able to get off a few more rounds before his death shot to the head. The pastor was hit in the spine and unfortunately, the bullet traveled, causing paralysis. Detective Spencer had been hit in the stomach. He was still recouping, and had retired as a result of his injury. Sean had died in that house. Alexis still had night-mares about it all, but it was getting better.

She kissed her husband and whispered, "I love you." She was glad that all this hadn't turned him away, but in fact, made them stronger. When she awoke in the hospital, he was right by her side. Looking around at everyone, she spotter her brother-in-law talking to Amber off to the side; they had been getting close. Terrance was around a lot more since she came home and the three of them attended Commander Sims' funeral. It was the first time she had seen Zavier shed tears when it came to him. He was healing and that was a good thing. They had become stronger, and that they both loved.

Getting herself out of her thoughts, Alexis mingled with her guests, making sure she spoke to everyone. When the DJ started playing, the party really started. She danced with Simone, her students, and finally landed in the arms of her husband to slow dance. The guests started to say goodnight around eleven. Amber, and the party crew she hired, began breaking the setup down. She tried to help but was shooed away by her newly promoted business manager. Zavier pulled a chair up next to her, putting her feet on his lap. He took her shoes off, slightly rubbing her feet. Alexis rubbed the side of his face.

She could have lost him, but she was so glad she hadn't. Thinking back over the last three years, but especially the last four months; she could easily see all she had lost. But what she gained in the end is what made her stronger.

The love that Zavier had given her was her strength to make sure she survived. Without him, things could have turned out so different. She never got her wedding but Zavier had promised to change that. They had chosen to exchange vows while she was recovering.

Reaching down she kissed her husband's ear. He laughed. It was that laugh, his dimples, and his heart. All his strong qualities that made her want to go down fighting. Alexis wanted to make sure that all victims of stalking had an opportunity to fight as well.

Stalking was one of the top unreported crimes. Alexis had learned the first stalking law wasn't passed until the 1990's.

She decided it was time to give stalking victims their lives back; the ones who dealt with being stalked and were silent. Although she was one of the lucky ones, there were so many victims, of both sexes, who had been or were currently being aggressively pursued by their stalkers and left defenseless most times. Especially if the stalker didn't cause physical harm according to the law.

Alexis decided to make sure that stalking wasn't left by the wayside any longer. She partnered with two self-defense instructors who would begin teaching the classes free of charge at her studio.

She also wanted to put things in place that would raise awareness. Detective Spencer even during his recuperation stage, was putting together a special task force with the guidance of the police chief. Spencer had given her his word that he would help once he was back to a hundred percent. Alexis wanted to work on making the stalking law stronger where the description actually protected its victims. One of her student's mother who was on the city council, agreed to host a rally that would garner the media and public's attention. The exposure was necessary. It was a small, but a huge start.

Picking up her shoes, she followed Zavier to the door. The party staff waved as they headed to their vehicle. Amber stepped around the couple. Waiting until Zavier locked the studio doors. The fall air was still warm. She finally felt her peace and joy. While they walked Amber to her car, she shook her head. Briefly her thoughts went to Sean. All of the terrible things had happened because of what he wanted—her. A woman who he had obsessed, killed, and eventually died for. Now, it was time to put it all behind her and start living her life, for once, not in fear.

THE END

If you or someone you know are being stalked. Please seek assistance.
For more information you can check out resources at the National
Victims of Crime Website
www.victimsofcrime.org

Made in the USA
Coppell, TX
10 May 2021